Totally Bou

CW00428225

Anthologies
Treble: Orchestrating Manoeuvres
Stand to Attention: Who Dares Wins
Wild Angels: Burning Rubber

Collections
Christmas Crackers: Candy Canes and Coal Dust
Bollywood: The Unwholesome Adventures of Harita

What's her Secret?
Breathe You In

What's her Secret?

BREATHE YOU IN

LILLY HARLEM

BREATHE YOU IN

Dedication

For my husband. Starting and ending each day with you makes my life perfect.

Chapter One

Kisses as soft as kitten's whiskers trickled down my back, fluttering, floating, spreading into the dip of my spine and onto the rise of my buttocks. I sighed and squirmed, just a little, inviting more of the blissful sensations I was being woken with.

Matt ran his finger down my side, from just below my breast into the hollow of my waist. So light it was barely a caress, so gentle it was hardly there. It tickled but in a good way, and I smiled, my cheek bunching on the pillow.

I could picture him hovering over me, ruggedly handsome, with his morning stubble heaviest on the indent of his chin. His broad shoulders and thick biceps would be tensing as he took his weight through his arms.

"Mmm, that's nice," I murmured, shifting my legs and wondering where his touch would travel next.

The duvet twisted around my ankles. I was naked, but my skin was warm—the night-time had done nothing to ease the English heatwave.

More sweet kisses, down my left leg this time and onto the back of my knee. I nibbled my bottom lip and forced my body still. I didn't know how much longer I'd be able to just lie there. My need for my husband was so big it was an energy that could give birth to stars. He was my everything, my world, my reason for breathing—the man I got out of bed for every morning.

I turned but kept my eyes closed, enjoying the remnants of sleep and the waft of his breath on my stomach, my breasts and my neck. I stretched my arms above my head, arched my back and pointed my toes, waiting to see where he would adore me next.

Was it Sunday? I hoped so. That way we could stay in bed all morning, worshiping each other's body, connecting our souls, feeling whole.

"Kiss me," I mumbled, tilting my chin and expecting to feel him pressing his lips to mine. "Matt, I want you." I smiled as I spoke and reached for him.

Birdsong filtered into my consciousness. The treetops outside my bedroom window were home to a family of doves, their coos a near constant melody. I pictured them, fat breasts, pale feathers, their devotion to each other endearing.

"Matt," I said again, flailing my arms.

As I'd spoken his name, the 'a' had caught in my throat. A strangled feeling clawed at my neck, and a rush of agony tumbled into my chest. I let my hands drop heavily onto the mattress.

My favorite part of the day was over. That empty moment between sleep and awake, horizontal and upright, before reality kicked in and dreams held court—when my memory hadn't remembered.

I shivered as kisses turned into a light breeze weaving through the open window. I kept my eyes tightly shut, hoping that might stop the usual tears from forming. But one persistent drip grew and seeped out anyway, its journey down my face unhindered by me. What difference did one more salty addition make when there'd been so many?

The usual leaden anvil of grief grew fat and ugly in my belly. All day and all night it would sit there, generating nausea, hopelessness and depression. I hated it, that damn grief. Why couldn't it let up, just for a few minutes? Why did it tail me like a ball and chain?

I tried to shift my thoughts back to a few minutes ago when Matt had been with me, kissing me, touching me. So many times he had, more than I could count. What I wouldn't do to be with him again, just once — just one night to say goodbye.

Was that too much to ask?

Of course it was.

A sudden rattle and the rev of an engine made me jump — the neighbors cutting their lawn at some ridiculous hour. I glanced at the clock. Well, it was gone ten, so I couldn't really complain. For a moment I thought I'd had a good, long sleep, but who was I kidding? The sun had been washing the eastern sky pink before I'd even lain down.

Bracing myself, I sat. This was the first hurdle of the day, getting out of bed. Most people rose, put their feet on the floor, and that was it. They were off. But that chunk of lead in my stomach... It made this bit especially hard. For a while, it had been impossible. It was just too damn heavy, and I'd stayed in bed for days, weeks, waiting for it to lighten.

It hadn't. Not in the least. But I'd learned how to get up again. It had to happen in careful stages. First I let the pain hit — I had to brace for that — then wait for it to settle. Once it had seeped into every pore and my brain had compartmentalized my reality into bite-sized snippets—yes, I'd be eating breakfast alone. No, he wouldn't be meeting me for lunch. Yes, the bed would still be empty tonight—then I sat and placed my hands behind myself with my elbows locked, kind of like a prop for my torso.

When I sat, that was when I saw him. The picture of us on our wedding day still had pride of place on my dressing table. I'd wondered about moving it, putting it on the windowsill or even downstairs, but I couldn't bring myself to. Perhaps it was torturous to have him smiling at me from a photograph when he never would again in real life. Maybe it was detrimental to the 'healing process'. But I couldn't help it. Looking at him in the morning was a compulsion. He'd been the start and end of my day for so many years. Why should I suddenly change that? How could I just 'put him away'?

I liked his eyes in that particular picture. We'd been lucky on our wedding day. It had been beautifully sunny, not a cloud in the sky. After our vows, we'd had photographs with family members then, sneakily, before the reception, the photographer had taken us around the back of the church to stand beneath an archway made up of delicate pink roses. It had matched the flowers in my bouquet and hair perfectly. Matt had hugged me close and told me I even smelled of roses.

I'd laughed and asked him if he could cope with thorns. He'd replied, "No marriage is without a few thorns, Katie, but for better or for worse, good times or bad, we're together now until death do us part."

He'd kissed me on my right temple, and the close-up shot had been taken. His eyes had been dreamy, soft, their dark depths mellow and his lashes casting shadows on his cheeks.

I recalled his smooth, clean-shaven chin against my face as clearly as I remembered my next words, spoken through a smile. "We'll still be together when we're old and gray and one hundred and ten."

How wrong I'd been.

I swung my feet to the floor and stared at my toenails — the dark pink nail varnish was hideously chipped — and forced myself to stand. There, that was it. I'd made it through the first painful moment of the day — only a million more to go.

I wandered into the bathroom, flicked on the shower and drowned out the sound of the mower. It was Saturday and I had the day off for a change so I didn't have to worry about getting into work and finding a smile to wear.

To start with it had been okay for me to be sad, quiet, closed in on myself. But since the first anniversary of Matt's accident had gone by ten months ago, I kind of got the feeling that people expected me to be 'getting on with my life', 'pulling myself together'. Really? A year and ten months to get over losing the man I'd spent over half a decade in love with, whose babies I'd wanted to carry and who I'd seen myself with for all eternity? It seemed it was. But I didn't have the energy to argue or try to justify the loss that still followed me everywhere, so I slapped on a smile, put a chirp in my voice and acted as if I cared about the goings-on in the shop.

The shower water was only just warm, but that was okay. The forecast had been for another scorcher, so starting off cool was a good plan. That's what Matt and I had done on our honeymoon in Thailand. We'd had cooling showers several times a day to lower our body temperatures, although sometimes, if he'd snuck in beside me, it had gotten pretty damn steamy in the bathroom, even with the faucet turned to cold.

I smiled at the delicious memory and stepped out, dried, then pulled on knickers and a thin sundress that had a built-in bra. The lemon-colored cotton was soft on my skin, and I recalled wearing it to a candlelit seafood dinner on the beach in Koh Samui. It'd fit a bit nicer back then. I'd filled it out properly. Now the material at the chest gaped slightly and it drowned the thin flare of my hips. But Matt had liked it, so I still wore it.

After piling my hair high, I wandered into the kitchen. As I put the kettle on I heard the letterbox rattle. My heart gave a familiar flip. I'd been waiting nearly eight weeks to hear back from Brian Davis. Would today be the day?

The brown hessian doormat held the usual bills and junk mail, but there was one slim white envelope with my name, Katie Lansdale, printed on the front. Quickly, I ripped it open, pulled out a sheet of paper and saw the words *Brian Davis, Private Detective*, written in bold print at the top.

I juddered in a breath, willed myself to keep calm, not to tear the paper in my urgency to unfold and read. My knees were weak so I headed into the kitchen, forced myself to lay the letter on the table, then made a cup of tea. The ritual of milk, squeezing the bag then stirring settled my movements, if not my nerves.

Questions without answers spun in my head like a sticky web, each one leading to the next, but not if I couldn't navigate the way. Would Brian have found anything out about the man who stomped through my thoughts? Had that man even survived this long? And if so, where was he now? In Britain? Europe? The other side of the world?

Eventually, tea made, kitchen door flung open to the back garden and the doves now pecking on the patio, I sat at our round kitchen table and unfolded the letter. The impulse to scan the sentences was strong, but I controlled it and started from the beginning, slowly, each word forming in my head.

Dear Mrs. Lansdale,

Further to our meeting on the 2nd of May, I have undertaken an investigation. Your request was unusual and did pose some ethical issues, but it seems fate has been on our side and I've found the man you seek.

He'd found him! I took a sip of tea, holding it over the table but away from the letter—my hand was shaking and I didn't want to spill a drop and risk blurring any precious words.

His name is Ruben Strong, and as you were already aware, he is thirty-three years old.

From what I can gather, he is doing extremely well health-wise. He is a UK resident and lives in Northampton, England, working as a curator in the town's park museum.

Since, as we discussed, address details cannot be revealed from health service documents, that is the extent of the information I can share. I trust that will satisfy your curiosity and have enclosed an invoice for the remainder of my fee, which should be settled within three weeks.

Yours sincerely,

Brian Davis

Personal Investigative Services

"Ruben Strong." The name sounded hard and alien on my lips and so different from melodic Matthew

Lincoln Lansdale. Yet he had a part of Matt. He *was* a part of Matt. I re-read the letter, soaking up the information anew. Northampton. That was only an hour away from Leicester. In fact, I was pretty sure the cosmetic shop I worked for had a branch in the town center there. Here was me thinking he could be anywhere in the world and he was only forty miles away.

And after all this time he was doing well.

That's good, isn't it? Yes, of course it is.

It meant something positive had come out of the senselessness of Matt's death. He was dead, but someone else was alive. Not just alive but 'doing extremely well'.

I read the letter twice more then picked up my tea and stood in the doorway, my shoulder huddled against the frame as I sipped and stared out at the garden. The doves sat side-by-side on the wooden bench, fussing each other's feathers. The sun beat down on my dry and crinkled lawn. I'd been unkind to it and had forgotten to put the sprinkler on night after night. Matt would have remembered. He'd been good like that.

But I didn't linger on the withered grass. Instead, I wondered if Ruben Strong was like his name — strong, big and tough. Not likely. Not if he'd needed a new heart and lungs. Maybe he'd had formidable strength once, but perhaps he'd always been sickly. He could have spent thirty-three years hoping someone would die in tragic circumstances so he'd get the chance of a normal life.

What must that feel like, to hope a stranger dies so you can live?

A bitter taste sat in my mouth. The tea wouldn't wash it away. It was the unfairness of it that was sour.

Why did anyone need to die or be ill in the first place? Young men, all in the prime of their lives, taken or about to be taken. I shut my eyes and tipped my face to the sky, wondered, *What divine creator would dream up such unfair scenarios?*

The sun beat down on me, unrelenting, unconcerned, just blistering. The neighbor thankfully turned off his cranky old mower.

I sighed then took a deep breath. The scent of summer filtered toward me—the pink roses that sat beneath the kitchen window were in full bloom. Matt had planted them on our first anniversary, and they were content in their south-facing position with the occasional jug of water thrown over them. I decided to cut several stems for the table. That was a normal thing to do, wasn't it? Have a vase of flowers in the kitchen?

I swapped my empty mug for a pair of scissors and set about snipping. The velvety petals were a delicate baby pink and smaller than usual roses. Their heads were dainty and didn't droop with weight. I gathered a dozen or so and stepped back into the shade of the house, already feeling a drip of perspiration in my cleavage.

After reaching for a glass vase then filling it with water, I dropped in the stems.

"Ouch. Bugger!" A thorn had caught on the inside of my index finger. Quickly, I sucked the drip of blood to take away the sting. As I stared at the haphazardly landed roses, an urge rushed into me. It was like getting hit by a moving object. It railroaded through my chest, swirled up that weight in my stomach—hurricane-style—and sent my heart rate rocketing.

I'd been a fool. A damn fool to think just knowing his name and where he worked would be enough.

Didn't I know anything about myself? Had I learned nothing about grief and its obsessive, dark, manipulative nature?

It was obvious I hadn't. Because if the thorn in our marriage had been Matt's death, the thorn in me now was that I'd be unable to rest until I'd seen Ruben Strong.

Chapter Two

After that first gush of desire to see Ruben Strong I didn't hang about. I applied a sweep of makeup, slotted in earrings and tamed my hair — regular things to do, and people always seemed glad I'd made the effort. Then I spent an hour in the stuffy heat of my car heading south on the motorway.

I knew I could be rash, impulsive and act without thinking. Matt had always said it was one of the things he adored about me — my sense of adventure — but I wasn't so sure what he'd think now. Was I being foolish and irresponsible? Setting myself up for more heartache when already I'd had quite enough?

I arrived in the park surrounding the museum and from a distance assessed the stern, brick-built building. I beat down a wave of nerves, wondering if I had the courage to go ahead with my plan.

A bench, the farthest edge of it in the shade of a huge pink rhododendron bush, offered a vantage point to the front of the museum and around the side toward a long drive and ornate metal gates. It didn't look particularly big — this collection of Northampton artifacts—nothing like the colossal London or Birmingham museums I'd been to. But it was a decent size—perhaps twenty or so sash windows over two levels, a green front door propped open with a big iron cobbler and a shallow roof that I suspected housed a dusty attic.

Summoning bravery and firming my resolution, I walked onto the gravel pathway, the crunch echoing from my soles to my ears. I darted my gaze about, looking for a man who'd suit the name Ruben Strong, but the hotness of the day had sent most people scurrying indoors. Two weeks into a heatwave and the novelty of sun worshiping had worn off for the majority of the population.

I took a seat at the end of the bench, in the shade, and watched as a couple of mothers with babes in prams approached. A gaggle of young children wandered behind them, licking melting ice creams and with their sunhats skew-whiff. They meandered lazily, not a care in the world, and for a moment, a pang of jealousy hit me. The desire to be like that again, absorbed and content with an ice cream and a trip to the park, was almost overwhelming. How long ago had it been since I'd felt carefree? How wrong I'd been when I'd truly thought pushing a pram with Matt's child inside it was part of my destiny.

They ambled off, leaving me alone as far as I could make out. The shrill call of what sounded like a peacock made me jump. I glanced over my shoulder, looking for it as I shooed a bug that was attracted to my lemony-colored dress. I hated big birds. The doves were fine, but anything bigger just gave me the creeps.

I should go into the park museum. That's why I'd come here—to see him. Nothing else, just to catch a glimpse, spot him from a distance, satisfy my curiosity about what he was like. But how would I know who he was? What if there were lots of men in their thirties working here? Maybe there were hundreds? Well, no, not hundreds, but perhaps three or four.

Taking a deep breath, I stood and tightened the strap of my handbag over my shoulder. I had to do it. What would be the point in turning around and driving all that way back up the motorway? It would be a waste of time and petrol, not to mention I'd hate myself when I got home for wimping out. I could just picture how my evening would go. There'd be the usual moping around and tears, forcing myself to eat — because people always asked if I had — but on top of that, there would also be moments when I'd just want to kick myself or bang my head against the wall in frustration. Then I'd be planning a trip back to Northampton tomorrow. I'd suffer this all over again.

No, I had no choice. I had to see this through. There wasn't one part of me that wouldn't. I at least had to try to get a peek of him, this man who had a piece of what was mine — a very important piece too.

I smoothed my dress, checked that the front hadn't tugged too low — which it was prone to these days — then walked toward the front entrance.

The peacock screeched again and I spotted it this time, out of the corner of my eye. It was parading on the lawn with its tail feathers spread and the dotty-eyed pattern shimmering in the sunshine. It appeared to be looking straight at me. Not only that, it was strutting toward the same door I was. I hurried a little, not wanting it to get too close but also quite fascinated by its haughty beauty and exquisite coloring.

The moment I stepped into the cool hallway, a dense silence enveloped me and thoughts of the peacock left my mind. Coolness drifted over my shoulders and clung there. I paused to let my eyes adjust after being in the dazzling outdoors and allowed the stillness that only museums seemed to emit soak into me.

"Good afternoon." A female voice.

I swallowed—my mouth was dry. I licked my lips and teeth. "Hello."

A middle-aged lady sat behind a low desk that held a cash register, several books of various sizes and a stack of leaflets, one of which she was offering my way.

"Would you like a map, dear?"

"Yes, thank you." I took the fold of glossy paper. I had words on my tongue and questions that sat heavily in my throat. Did she know Ruben Strong? Did he indeed work here? Was he on duty today? How was he?

But I said nothing. Instead, I pressed my lips together and bided my time. What if she said yes and quickly went to get him? What the hell would I say? I didn't want to speak to him. I just needed to see him from afar. To be sure he was fit and healthy, and that what he had of Matt's was serving him well, and that he was serving it well too. That was important to me.

"Most people start through that way," the lady behind the counter said, pointing to her left.

I noticed she had a name badge with a tiny picture of the museum and the name *Ethel* next to it in bold black print.

"Okay, thanks."

"Hot out there, isn't it?" She picked up another leaflet and fanned it in front of her face.

"It is, yes. Do I, er, have to pay or anything?"

"No, no, dear, it's all free. Go and have a look around and keep out of the midday sun. You know what they say about mad dogs and Englishmen, but I think these last few weeks have converted us all, don't you?"

"Yes, it's certainly been warm."

She smiled, then a phone on the table trilled to life. "Oh, excuse me, dear. You have a nice little look around now. Any questions, just ask a member of staff." She picked up the phone. "Hello, Ethel speaking... Oh yes, of course... I'll man this desk while you sort that out then... The 1940s display? Yes, ten minutes. Okay."

The first room I came to held several big dark wooden dressers stuffed with trinkets. I gazed absently at them—jewelry boxes, compact mirrors, pillboxes. They were pretty enough, but not what I'd come to see. On a stack of shelves were shoes and boots of various sizes and in an array of disrepair.

I hung around for a few minutes to make it look as if I were there as a genuine museum-goer, should anyone be watching me. After reading the small brass plaques beneath a half dozen portraits of stuffy-looking ladies in old-fashioned dresses, I moved through to the next room.

Taxidermy seemed to be the main theme in this high-ceilinged area. Instantly my guts rolled and the hairs on the back of my neck spiked. I hurried past a glass cabinet holding a snarling fox with milky eyes, then winced at several stuffed birds perched on twigs that looked like they'd been snagged from the park outside. I quickly exited through a dark doorway that had an enormous snowy-white owl glaring down from the top frame, not caring that I hadn't lingered to appreciate whatever it was that dead, stuffed animals were supposed to offer.

I suppressed a shudder. The thought of being packed full from the inside like that was gross, as was doing it to animals that had once been living, breathing things. What kind of person picked taxidermy as a job? Who would want to work in a place that housed those things? Ruben Strong obviously didn't mind them, not if this was where he spent his days. Perhaps he was a creep—a real weirdo. The sort who had odd collections of bizarre things— rare birds' eggs with the insides sucked out or famous people's toenail clippings. *Yuk, I hope not.* I wanted him to be normal, to be appreciative of what he had and to be enjoying his second chance at life by doing healthy, respectful things.

Absently I stared at a collection of black-and-white pictures showing the Northamptonshire countryside being farmed by horse and plow and the crops picked by hand. He didn't have to be a saint—that was expecting too much—but he had to be good and honorable, otherwise what was the point?

I still hadn't encountered anyone on my journey through the silent rooms. It really wasn't the busiest of museums. It was a little dusty, too—a bit worn around the edges.

Beside a set of stone grinding wheels was an old oil radiator—as much an antique as the artifacts it was designed to keep warm in the winter. I noticed the paint peeling beside the window frame. An insipid green, its curling flakes revealed a dusty brick-like substance.

I moved through to the next room. It was dark, the walls painted black, and in the corner was what looked like a bunker and some kind of corrugated iron shelter. A sudden wail—an air-raid siren—blasted out of a speaker above me. The lights flashed on and off, and a deafening boom rattled across the ceiling and pounded up through the soles of my feet.

I clutched my handbag. Stepped backwards. *What the hell…?*

A loud voice hollered out. "Northampton during the Blitz. This is what it was like to live in the town in 1943."

"Oh, shit, really?" My heart was galloping, and my bearings had slipped. I couldn't see the way out, other than the archway I'd just come through. There was no obvious exit that would keep my journey progressive through the museum.

Another loud bang, followed by whizzing and an explosion that clanked several wall-hanging gas masks and jerry cans against one another.

I had to get out of there. It smelled musty, and it was so dark and loud I could hardly think.

Spinning, I came face to chest with another person.

"Sorry," I said, the need to flee now overwhelming. "I'm just…" I glanced left and right. Staggered slightly.

"Hey, are you okay?" He cupped my elbows, steadied me.

I looked up through the shadows into dark eyes. "Er, yes, I think so. It just made me jump, that's all. It's a bit loud."

"I'm sorry. It's supposed to be noisy but this is too much."

"Yes, it's ear-splitting."

Bomb sounds were raining down on us with gusto. Screams and shouts were mixed into the soundtrack now, adding to the chaos.

"Which, er, way…?" I asked.

"Through the army camouflage curtain, just there."

Shadows sliced across his face but were lost momentarily when the lights flared again, simulating explosions. I reckoned he was about my age, maybe a little older. He had a straight, long nose, wide mouth and a flat, brown mole on his right cheek.

"Okay." I was about to step away but realized I'd placed my hand on his chest, right next to a small badge that had a picture of the museum in the left hand corner. Also on that badge, written in bold black letters, was the name *Ruben*.

I snapped my hand away. Had I felt the thud of a heart beating beneath my palm? Panic raced through my body, starting in my fingers and shooting up my arm. It went into my lungs and belly, weakening my knees and softening my spine.

It was him. I knew it was. How many Rubens could possibly work here? Not only that, I'd touched him. Hell, he was still touching me. This wasn't my plan, not at all. No way.

Gasping, I moved back, still staring at his badge, at his chest. Beneath that neat white shirt, his skin and bones, was Matt—Matt's heart and lungs. Beating. Inflating. The heart that had loved me so much.

Oh, God.

My plan had gone terribly wrong. I was only supposed to see Ruben from a distance, not speak to him, definitely not touch him.

"I have to…" I said, bumping into the plastic-molded bunker and the side of the Anderson shelter. "Go." I straightened, just…my body didn't feel like mine. I was shaking, hot and cold, my brain infused with fear and fascination.

"Are you okay?"

"Fine."

What the hell was the matter with my vision? I couldn't peel my attention away from his chest, his name badge, the way his shirt hung down, flat against his long, lean body. It was buttoned at the top, the collar sitting neat against his neck. There was no scar that I could make out, but there would be one. I knew that much.

"Are you sure?" he asked over the din.

"Yes." I managed to move toward the exit he'd indicated. "You really should get this volume turned down before you give someone a heart attack."

He laughed as another flash filled the room. "The kids love it, but yes, you're right. I was actually just fiddling with it." He turned and disappeared into the room with the plow and the grinding wheels.

I stared at the space he'd just occupied—at a place in the world a piece of Matt, that wasn't ash and dust, had just been. Tears filled my eyes. I clenched my hand into a fist, imagining I was trapping those beats of his heart I'd possibly just felt. I needed them. They were mine. They used to beat for me and only me—so he'd said.

Dashing at a tear that had over-spilled, I rushed from 'Northampton in the Blitz' and found myself in a room dedicated to shoes and the local cobbler factories. But it held no interest for me. I just needed to get the hell out of there. Confusion swirled inside me. Guilt poked at me like an accusing finger, at the same time as a need to know more about Ruben tugged me. I shouldn't be here. I *had* to be here.

Next was a narrow corridor lined with eerie-looking mannequins dressed in dusty, stiff outfits. I rushed past them, and as I did so, I heard the distant bombs stop falling. I needed fresh air and to take stock of what had just happened back there.

Thankfully, the next section spat me out at reception. A wide set of steps with brass grippers hugging a thready, bottle-green carpet offered the way up to more display rooms—Northampton's sporting achievements, the Romans, the canal network.

"Are you going up, dear?" Ethel, the lady on reception, grinned at me. Her hair was shifting. She'd turned on an electric fan and it was catching gray wisps and floating them over her cheek.

"Er, no, I'm done, thanks."

"Oh, okay." She looked a little put out. "But will you come back another day? You've only seen half of the exhibits."

"Yes, perhaps. Is there anywhere around here I can get a cup of tea?"

Her face softened. "Yes, of course, go right out of the door, past the aviary and the bandstand and there's a café. You should be able to find some shade."

"Okay, that's great. Thanks."

Chapter Three

The sun was still relentless, but I hardly noticed it now. I was in turmoil. When I'd got out of bed this morning, I'd had no idea where Matt's heart was or who it was serving. And now, only hours later, I'd actually rested my hand over it.

I walked, unsteadily, past the side of the museum, the deep gravel hampering my steps. I could hear the aviary the receptionist had mentioned — the happy chatter of sociable little birds. As I turned the corner, a pathway edged with large-domed wire cages led toward a distant bandstand set on a wide lawn.

A cup of tea was just what I needed, preferably with a dash of brandy in it. It was so strange to come face-to-face with Matt's recipient like that — almost as if he were waiting for me here and all I'd had to do was come and find him. Of course, that was rubbish and fanciful thinking. If that stupid exhibition room hadn't been so loud, I would never have even stepped back into him. We would have had nothing to talk about. We'd never have met.

I paused, gripped the railings that lined the path and stared into a cage full of zebra finches that were darting about. Did Ruben know anything about Matt? Did he know the heart that now beat so strongly in his chest came from a fine man who had been loyal and kind, had hated injustice and adored West Ham United? Had the transplant team told him that Matt had always dreamed of being a father, of being a grandfather too? That he'd disliked cheese of any description and could listen to U2 for months at a time in his car without bothering to change the disk?

Movement caught my attention.

Shit.

The peacock was right next to me. There wasn't an arm's length between us—or a leg if I had to kick it to protect myself. The damn thing had its tail feathers spread into an enormous shimmering fan shape and it was making a strange snorting sound.

Its black beady gaze was fixed firmly on me.

"Shoo," I said, pressing up against the railings. "Go away."

I flicked my handbag toward it, but that seemed to enrage the fierce-looking bird further. It shook its arc of colorful feathers and scraped its foot on the floor as if preparing for attack. Its beak appeared sharp and wicked, hooked at the end, prehistoric almost. I wondered how fast they could run. Were they like emus and could sprint for miles?

Suddenly it tipped its head back and made an awful screeching sound. Its little black tongue waggled as it cried out its battle scream several times over. The murderous sound made my ears ring.

"Get out of here, Chester. Stop bullying the visitors." Sharp snapping came from my right, someone clapping hard and fast.

I flicked my bag at the peacock again and stepped away, not daring to take my eyes off the ferocious creature.

"Go. Go…be off with you."

The peacock shuffled backward and in its place stood Ruben Strong.

Fight or flight warred within me. I should have run away but was compelled to stay put. The adrenaline rush gave me a giddy sensation. "I am sorry about this," he said with a smile. "You're really not having the relaxing time we hope our visitors to the museum will enjoy."

"What's the matter with that thing?" I asked shakily, now unsure whether or not to stare at Ruben or the peacock that was still eyeing me up as if I were his next meal. Part of me was hugely embarrassed that I'd been cornered by a damn bird, the other part hardly believed that the man who I'd come only to catch a glimpse of was standing before me, again.

"Oh, he's just grumpy. His peahen is sitting on eggs, though whether it will come to anything this late in the season I don't know, plus they're terrible parents." Ruben turned and gave a final flick of his hands, sending the rogue peacock on its way. "I think the heat must be bothering him too."

It strutted back toward the entrance of the museum, huge tail still spread, haughty neck bobbing.

"Well, thanks. It was about to mug me." I took a deep breath and set my attention on Ruben as he tipped his head back and laughed. He had dark-brown hair, a fraction over-long, and it fell past his ears and down his neck. He also had sideburns, again a bit too long, as was the fashion at the moment.

"Unless you've got a stash of sunflower seeds in your bag, he wouldn't have mugged you."

"Mmm, I'm not convinced."

I managed a small smile. Ruben's was infectious, wide and genuine. It created tiny crinkles at the corners of his eyes and showed a neat set of teeth, though his right canine protruded a fraction. I felt a hesitant calmness wash through me—the claustrophobia of the museum and the shock of accidentally bumping into Ruben was fading. We could talk a little. Right?

"They're actually considered symbols of immortality," Ruben said, glancing at the departing bird.

"Why?"

He turned back to me and slipped on a pair of shades. "Apparently the ancients believed peacock flesh didn't decay after death." He shrugged. "Which of course, it does, but it's a nice thought."

Again I looked at his chest. His name badge was at an angle. Not all flesh decayed after death. Some lived on. Some could allow others to live on.

"Er…is the café this way?" I asked, my voice croaky.

"Yes, are you meeting someone there?" He skimmed his attention over my left hand.

I was clutching the strap of my handbag over my breast.

"Your husband?"

Instinctively I looked at my wedding band. I'd been unable to remove it. In my mind I was still married. Matt was still my husband. We hadn't divorced. He'd gone, but not because he'd wanted to.

"My husband is dead."

Ruben shifted his head back, as though the bluntness of my words had been a quick slap to his face.

It was the first time I'd said it like that. As a rule I skirted around the question — not that it had been asked many times. I wasn't in the habit of meeting new people. Usually I preferred to say Matt had had an accident or he'd passed away — or that I was a widow.

With Ruben, however, something had just made me say it how it was. Matt was dead. There was no way to fluff it up. Death didn't come in a soft pink box with flowers and perfume. It was black and hard and seeped into every cell of your body. But Ruben knew that, right? He'd faced death. He must have. Although he was the lucky one. He'd stared it in the face then lived to tell the tale.

"I'm really sorry," he said, removing the shades he'd only just put on and folding in their thin arms. He shifted his feet and stared down at the gravel. "That's tragic."

I bit my bottom lip. Did he really think it was? If Matt hadn't died, he wouldn't be alive. My tragedy was Ruben Strong's salvation. "Yes, it is."

I twisted and turned to the ornate white bandstand. Several stout men with brass instruments appeared to be getting ready to perform

"Can I buy you a drink?" Ruben asked suddenly. "Tea, coffee, or maybe even a Coke or something, if it's too hot for tea, that is?"

I looked at him again. This was so far off what I'd intended.

"To apologize," he said, "for your mishaps with the bombs and the killer peacock. Not the best impression of our old establishment." He held out his hand. "I'm Ruben, by the way. Ruben Strong."

I hesitated for a moment then reached out. Warm flesh surrounded my fingers, hard and firm, but with a gentleness about it. Alive flesh, flesh that was nourished with oxygen and vitamins and everything else it needed by Matt's strong organs.

"Katie Lansdale," I said. Did he know Matt's surname? No, of course not. Anonymity was a buzzword the transplant coordinator had slung around constantly, but even so, I looked for a reaction.

There was nothing, not even a flicker.

"Pleased to meet you, Katie."

"Yes, please," I said, "I mean, yes please to the cup of tea. It would be very much appreciated."

He smiled, released my hand then gestured toward the bandstand. "The café is just beyond there. We should be able to sit in the shade. They've moved the outside seats beneath the cover of trees. They don't normally, but it's just been too hot."

"I agree." I stepped forward, and he kept pace with me.

"Is this your first visit to the park and the museum?" he asked.

"Yes."

"What's brought you here?"

"I'm thinking of moving to Northampton."

Jesus, why did I say that?

"Where from? I mean…where are you living now?"

"Leicester."

"Not too far, then."

"No, not really." I hesitated "Do you like living here?"

He stooped, picked up a crushed can littering the pathway, then tossed it into a nearby bin. Perfect shot. "Yes, very much. The town is reasonable for shopping, the property cheap enough, and I like to catch the train to London every now and then to visit the museums or go and see a show."

"Museums are your thing, then?"

He laughed, slipped his shades back on. "They are these days. I used to be based nearby at Silverstone, the racetrack, helping out with McLaren's Formula One team. But I had to cut back my hours about five years ago." He paused. "Something came up and I needed to slow down, take a bit of time out."

I wondered whether or not to question him further. Clearly what had happened was his heart problem. No good having a dodgy ticker and working in a high-energy, fast-paced racing environment. That would finish him off pretty quickly. I decided against any probing. It didn't seem polite, and I wasn't sure if I was ready for details. "And you like working in the museum here?"

He looked at me and pushed his hand through his hair, feathering it between his fingers. Was he surprised that I hadn't questioned him about his drastic career change?

"Yeah, it's okay. Could do with some cash spent on it, but the people are nice — the ones that work here and who visit." He grinned. "Take you, for example."

I glanced down at my dress, made sure it wasn't gaping and showing too much of my skin. It was okay.

"So, um, what line of work are you in?" he asked as we walked past the end of the row of birds and onto the lawn.

"I'm a sales assistant in a cosmetic store. Not the most taxing of jobs or one with enormous room to climb the corporate ladder, but I like it."

"Sounds interesting." He shoved his hands into his trouser pockets.

"It's okay. The people are nice, and like you just said, that makes all the difference. Plus, I'm passionate about organic beauty and reducing our carbon footprint, which is what Skin Deep is all about."

"Oh, I've heard of them." He lightened his voice. "In fact, I got my mother one of their gift sets for her birthday this year. She's all for saving the planet and steering away from chemicals. I bought it from the branch in town."

"That's where I'm going to be working." Since when had I become a liar? I'd never told such whoppers before. It was completely out of character for me.

"The one on Abington Street?"

"Yes, that's it." Was it? Bloody hell, I had no idea.

"And why are you moving?"

A trombone blasted out a low note, and I waited until the sound had dissipated before speaking. "I feel ready for a change." As the words came out of my mouth, I realized that I did. I wasn't really lying. I was just speaking from my soul. I needed a change, a new start. I was fed up of being the young widow people still felt sorry for but thought was ready to date again. I needed to move away from the bricks and mortar that had played home to my nights of crying and sobbing, of staring into space wondering 'why me'. Yes, I needed something else—something other than grief and loss.

This 'something else' caught my breath, and I paused and turned to the band. Unable to keep moving in the direction I was going. A new tilt had been put on my world. Was my path about to change? Had I come to a crossroads?

Yes. I had a choice to make.

That new knowledge was like getting socked in the stomach. It made my head spin and my fists clench.

"They play every afternoon," Ruben said, also stopping and gesturing to the congregation of suited, elderly gentlemen settling with their instruments in the bandstand.

I was glad of the moment to collect myself. Let that new, positive feeling find a place to settle. It was too delicate to examine right now. I'd have to sift through it later, untangle the threads and scrutinize the options. Carefully, I put a lid on it, not completely, just as if I were letting a pot simmer on the stove.

"That's nice," I said. "That they like to play." Now we were closer and I could see that a coat of paint wouldn't do the bandstand any harm. The color was peeling and there was some rust showing on the ornate swirls around the pillars.

He laughed. "You haven't heard them yet."

I looked up at him, watched the way he touched the fuzz of hair that ran in front of his ears.

"So do you really want tea or would you prefer something cold?" he asked.

"Tea is perfect."

"Coming right up." He pointed to a scattering of chairs and tables beneath several ancient oak trees. About half of the tables were occupied. "You go and grab us a seat, and I'll join you in a minute."

I did as Ruben had told me, pleased to have a moment alone with my new imposturous thoughts. It was only just cooler in the shade. There was no breeze. The leaves in the trees above me were perfectly still.

I watched Ruben as he went to the window of the café rather than going inside — kind of like a walk-through for park-goers. He was the only customer, and within a minute he was walking over, heading my way carrying a tray — no time at all for me to examine that bubbling pan of ideas.

Forcing myself not to stare at his tall frame and the way his long legs made short work of the distance between us, I turned my attention to a chip of wood on the bench, poked at it with my thumbnail until it spiked upward in a little splinter.

"I wasn't sure if you'd join me in a cream bun, but I bought a couple anyway." He placed the tray down, sat opposite me, then propped his shades on the top of his head.

The tray held a can of Coke and a white teapot with a stringy label hanging out from beneath the lid—PG Tips. A matching cup, saucer and little jug of milk sat at its side. On a larger plate were two decadent cakes—thick choux pastry bursting with cream, smothered in snow-white icing and topped with glossy red cherries.

"They look calorie-laden," I said.

"I skipped lunch." He shrugged. "I don't normally skip meals or indulge in this much cholesterol, but they say a little of what you fancy does you good."

"Mmm, you're right." The cakes were calling to me. I couldn't remember when I'd last had a cream bun or even had the desire for one. Having an appetite was off my radar these days.

"Do you take sugar?" He pushed several sachets my way.

"No thanks, but yes, I think I will join you in a cake."

"Good," he said, passing me a saucer with *Park Café* written on it. "I would have felt piggy eating alone."

I took a bun and, unable to resist, sank my teeth into it. "Oh wow," I said, covering my mouth with my hand as the combination of cool cream and light pastry blended with soft icing melting on my tongue.

"Good eh?" His eyes widened, and he bit into his own.

"Seriously amazing." I bit off another chunk. What a delicious treat.

He chewed then swallowed, looked at me and grinned. "I like a girl who can appreciate food."

"Well, I don't normally…" He'd think I was mad if I said I didn't normally enjoy food, just forced myself to eat to keep people off my back about my weight loss. "I mean, I don't normally indulge in cream, but like you said, a little of what you fancy." I put the cake down and poured my tea, added a splash of milk.

He popped the ring pull on his can of Coke and took several deep swallows. His Adam's apple bobbed as he glugged, and he shut his eyes, as though appreciating the cold drink.

I sipped my tea then continued to eat.

"So when are you moving here?" he asked.

"In a week." My mouth wasn't my own. It was running away with me. In a bloody week, what was I on about? Moving house so fast was impossible, wasn't it?

"That soon?"

"Yes, I'm going to look at a flat later."

The band started, and we both glanced over. Some deep base tune that I vaguely recognized had started up. They were all lies — the flat thing and the job thing, but perhaps I could turn it into reality. Actually make Northampton my new start. My something else. Who was to say I couldn't go and look at a flat before I headed back up the motorway? I could, if I wanted to.

Damn, I couldn't keep a rein on these thoughts. They were like a horse desperate to get out of the stable. I should feel terrible but I didn't. It felt good — this boost, this propeller starting up beneath me. And besides, what did it matter, these untruths? It wasn't as if I was going to see Ruben again, not after today, and if they helped me take a brave new step, then that was okay.

"Whereabouts is the flat?" Ruben asked.

"Er, I'm not sure, the estate agent is taking me there."

"I live just a walk from here," Ruben said, gesturing back toward the museum. "I have great views over the park."

"Oh, one of the big terraces?" I'd seen them lining the main road. Tall, majestic town houses with pillared front porches and wide stone steps.

"Yes, most of them, like mine, are flats. The residents use the park as their garden. Perfect, no maintenance."

"And what a garden." I finished my food then licked the cream and icing off my fingers. A sugar rush would hit in a minute.

"You've got a bit..." He pointed at my face then stroked the corner of his mouth.

"Oh, have I?" I poked out my tongue, felt a stray bit of cream and licked it off.

Ruben watched me then slid his tongue over the seam of his lips, as though also checking for cream and crumbs.

"That was delicious," I said. "I probably shouldn't have, though." I rubbed my flat stomach.

"I don't think you need to worry about calories, Katie. You look great." He glanced away, toward the band again.

I wasn't sure, but I thought a little color rose on his cheeks as he took another drink.

I concentrated on my tea, grateful for its familiar, soothing effect. It was as if I were dreaming. Here I was with Ruben Strong, who Matt had donated something so vital to, and we were having tea in the park and listening to a brass band as though we were a couple of olden-day colonials.

My life had certainly taken a strange turn. And with all these new thoughts swirling in my head about moving here, moving to the town where Ruben lived, bizarre didn't seem a powerful enough word.

"So what did you think of the museum?" Ruben asked.

"It was nice."

"Nice... That's not very descriptive." He smiled.

"Okay." I poked at the splinter again. "I thought the shoes were quaint, the stuffed animals creepy and the Blitz room scared the crap out of me."

"That's more like it. Proper feedback."

"You should get rid of the animals," I said.

"I wish that was my decision. I hate them too. Not so bad in the summer, but in the winter, when it's dark early and the lights are on low, their eyes seem to glow and follow you around the room."

I suppressed a shudder. "Yuck, see what I mean — creepy."

"It would be much cooler to have some dinosaurs," he said. "I was mad on dinosaurs as a kid. To me that was the only thing I thought museums should house. Of course, there are lots of arguments against that."

"Yes, I suppose." I paused. "So what did I miss? I didn't go upstairs."

"Loads of stuff about the Saints. That's the town's rugby team. A pile of old Roman coins and bits of china that have been found over the years. The really interesting stuff is in the attic, including some things that have recently been donated from the Althorpe Estate."

"Where Princess Diana grew up?" Now that impressed me.

"Yes, it's just down the road from here and they've given us some pictures that were painted by her father. They just need cleaning up and reframing. That's been one of my jobs this last month or so—that and making the information plaques to go next to them. They'll go to auction in a year—to raise money for charity—but until then, we get them."

"Sounds an interesting project for you."

He shrugged. "My life was more interesting when I had to supervise changing four tires on a Formula One car in less than fifteen seconds, but I'm not complaining."

Of course he wasn't, because at least he had a life. Unlike Matt. I felt a familiar prickle in my eye, a rogue tear forming. Damn. Just when I'd been walking along my emotional tightrope so steadily. I reached into my bag for a tissue and dabbed my eye. It was the unfairness of Matt's death that hit me like a bolt of lightning sometimes—kind of like having someone twang that tightrope I was stepping so carefully on and making it shake and wobble and disrupt my balance.

Then again, today was turning out to be more than I'd expected. In fact, sitting here with Ruben Strong had thrown up a cascade of emotions I was trying to keep in. I feared I was about to lose the battle. Soon I would be overwhelmed.

"You okay?" he asked.

"Must be a bit of hay fever," I said and glanced at my watch. "I should get going, you know, to meet this estate agent."

"Yes, of course."

I stood, needing to get away from him, though also wanting to stay. But I couldn't, not if I wanted to maintain any kind of composure. Just ten more seconds of keeping the lid on, that was all I needed. I could do that. Yes. I could. "But thanks for the cake, and for…you know, saving me from the Blitz and the peacock."

"Not every day I get the chance to be a knight in shining armor." He smoothed his hand over his shirt. "Well, not armor, but white cotton anyway."

Tucking my handbag against my side and pushing my hair behind my ears, I stepped away.

"Katie."

I turned.

Ruben was standing now, hands in his pockets, shoulders a little slumped. He prodded a clump of dry grass with his shoe. "Would you, er… Would you like to go out for a drink sometime, you know, when you move here? And I'd be happy to show you the sights, in the area, help you get your bearings. Not that there's many sights now you've seen the museum and the park…"

He looked awkward and handsome, bashful and confident all at the same time. A strange feeling of longing tugged in my chest. Longing for what?

"There's lively places in town," he went on, "or quiet country pubs just outside—whatever you prefer."

I said nothing. I probably appeared frozen, like a rabbit stuck in a flashlight beam, but inside I was in turmoil. Ruben Strong was asking me on a date. Shit, how the hell had that happened? What on earth would my friends think? What the hell would Matt have thought?

"Just a drink?" Ruben said, "No pressure, not a date or anything. I'm just guessing you won't know many people, what with you just moving here and everything."

Not a date. Not a date, I repeated to myself. Okay then, I could handle that. I wasn't ready to actually go out with a bloke again. Was I?

Oh, the questions I was being faced with this afternoon. And here was another one. Did I want to spend more time with Ruben?

That was an easier one, because who was I kidding? A part of Matt was inside this man who stood before me. How could I not want to spend time with him? It could be just what I needed, a feeling of connection.

"That would be lovely," I managed. Damn, I'd never be able to tell anyone about this. They'd think I was off my rocker.

Ruben grinned. "Great. Look. Here's my museum card, it's got my personal mobile on it. Call me when you get settled in and we'll head out."

I took the small blue card that held the same picture as his badge and a mobile number beneath his name. I swallowed tightly. "Okay. I'll do that."

Will I? Will I really?

Then sanity managed to break through grief and slap me around the face for my madness, would I actually call him? No, surely not. My heart and soul had taken all the beatings they could cope with, enough to last an eternity. There was no way I'd subject myself to the agony of going for a drink with Ruben Strong. It was just the heat of the moment making me do this—the confused state I was in.

"I'll call you next weekend then," I said, slipping the card into the front pocket of my bag.

It was official. I'd gone mad.

Chapter Four

"Katie, are you absolutely sure? I mean, I think it's wonderful that you've made this decision, but will you be okay? You don't know anyone in Northampton."

I stared at Melanie—my boss and good friend of seven years—and fiddled with my wedding ring, twirling it around and around. "Yes, I've been thinking about a move, a fresh start, for a while now. I just didn't say anything to anyone."

"Well, I can see that it could be good for you, and Northampton isn't too far away at all. You'll still be able to visit us, plus we have Felicity's wedding in a few months, so there's the hen party and all of that…" She trailed off. People often did when weddings were mentioned around me.

"I can easily come back for that. I wouldn't miss it."

"Good." She smiled. "And what about the house? Are you going to sell it?"

"No, I'm going to rent it out. I can't quite bring myself to sell. Not yet."

"Of course." She pulled her eyebrows low and nodded.

"A letting company has been round. They said they had several people on their books who would snap my hand off to live there. Very popular area apparently." I kept my tone light and conversational.

Melanie nodded again. "And what about somewhere to stay in Northampton? I'll have to give the Abington Street Branch all of your details and they'll need an address."

"That's sorted." I hesitated. I didn't want her to think I'd been too presumptuous about her allowing me to transfer branches of Skin Deep, but the truth was I would have changed jobs to get to Northampton.

After I'd left Ruben on Saturday, I'd become a woman on a mission. Each step across that lawn away from him had been like adding structure to feeling alive again. I'd known by the time I'd gotten back to my car that agreeing to go for a drink with him the next weekend had been absolutely the right thing to do. And no matter what obstacles were in my way, I would be living in Northampton when that happened. It was the only thing I could do to make up for the lies that had flowed like syrup from my mouth — lies that had been as sticky as they'd been a prophecy. "I've seen a place to rent. It's cute, has character and is in a lovely part of town. I've put down a deposit already."

She raised her eyebrows, and I knew I had indeed been too presumptuous. She might be a close friend, but she was also my boss.

I shrugged and smiled. "I was there — looking around, you know, visiting the shops, the parks — and I saw a flat that called to me from an estate agent window. The place is empty and the deposit fully refundable if for some reason it's not okay for me to transfer. So nothing is lost if it's not a possibility."

The deposit wasn't refundable on my new little one-bed place that overlooked the north section of the park and into a school playground, but that didn't matter. Money hadn't been an issue for me since Matt's death. He'd known his job was risky and had been well-insured. Plus, the mortgage had automatically been paid off and I'd had a substantial lump sum placed in our — or rather my — bank account from his company. A few years of his wages, to be exact. No, money wasn't one of my concerns, not that that had ever been a comfort. Not really.

"Oh, well," Melanie said with a sad smile. "In that case, it's just a matter of me making a phone call. I know they're short because they have two on maternity leave and what with everyone wanting holidays this time of year. I'm sure they'll say the sooner you can start, the better."

"Really?" It would be great if I could stay working at a Skin Deep branch. It was a job I could do with my eyes closed and I really didn't need to use up valuable brainpower learning anything new at the moment. My thoughts, since Saturday, had been too full of Ruben — not just that he had something of Matt's inside him, but his smile and the way he'd blushed when giving me his number. I felt drawn to him, to seeing him again. I hoped it wouldn't be long until I did. "I would like to be there by next Monday, really."

"A week today?"

"Yes." I flattened my lips together determinedly. It was the only way to do this, in one quick swoop while I still had the courage.

"Oh, well, of course." She looked surprised, maybe a little hurt too. "We'll have to round everyone up for goodbyes on Friday."

I softened my expression, put on the mask I knew I would wear on Friday. "That sounds great. We should head to that new Indian restaurant Felicity was raving about."

"Oh, yes, that sounds lovely." Melanie picked up her phone. "I'll make that call, then. Let you know once things are confirmed. But you know…we will miss you terribly."

* * * *

My last week in Leicester had gone by in a blur. Everyone had been surprised but supportive of my decision, and there'd been lots of hugging and tears at the end of our meal on Friday night. I couldn't help but wonder if my colleagues were a bit relieved to see me going. When I was around, I got the feeling they always worried about saying the wrong thing and upsetting me. Mentioning their own husbands or plans for the weekend were often said with hesitancy. It all meant I had to appear enthusiastic and interested if they were to continue—and I *was* interested—sort of.

Those thoughts made me even more determined to look at the bigger picture. I needed a new life with people who didn't know me as the sad young woman who'd lost the love of her life one rainy Thursday in September. It had been an ordinary day, nothing remarkable except the promise of seeing each other that evening for dinner and a cuddle on the sofa.

The difference one phone call could make.

I shoved my last box of clothes into the back of my car and slammed the boot, relieved when the catch caught and the glass didn't shatter. There was so much rammed into that small vehicle—the majority of my possessions, except for furniture. That could stay. I was renting our house as a furnished property and my new flat was freshly decked out and looked like something from an Ikea catalog.

I was just taking clothes, books, photos, a few ornaments and kitchen bits and pieces. Also, to make me feel a little more as if the place were mine, a pile of cushions and bedding. Basically, a Vauxhall Corsa held what was left of my life. That wasn't a thought I wanted to dwell on, not today, the first day of my new beginning. So I jumped in, revved the engine and pulled away from Hemmingway Close.

Heading out of Leicester on the dual carriageway, I then turned left, toward the cemetery. I didn't intend to linger, just go and tell Matt what I was doing. It seemed like the right thing to do.

After parking up, I donned a large, floppy sunhat and a pair of shades, clicked my car locked before stepping into the silence.

The cemetery was enormous and on a graduated slope leading up to the crematorium. Although the sun was hot, it didn't heat me—not really—because this wasn't a place I liked coming to, even though on occasions I was drawn here. Painful memories, images of the agony on Matt's parents' faces, my parents' faces, Matt's best friend and wife, his work colleagues all came to mind. Of course, their images had been blurred. I'd been crying.

Weaving what was sadly a familiar path through a section of older tombs, I walked toward the small copse. There was a brand-new gravestone there. A big stone angel with outstretched wings and praying hands. The arc of wings reminded me of the peacock, Ruben clapping and scaring it away. What would I have done if he hadn't appeared? Let the damn thing bully me? No, surely not, I was made of tougher stuff. I'd have whacked it with my bag and ran. Yes, that's what I'd have done.

But I was glad he had shown up.

I carried on walking. Most graves had flowers on them. Some were fake and looked bright and happy despite the continuing hot weather, some were so old and dead they were just potpourri lying in cellophane. Others looked fresher, although they wouldn't for long. Many graves had small toy animals sitting next to them—a few held photographs or candles in jars.

When I reached the black, shiny stone inscribed with the words, *Matthew Lincoln Lansdale 1982-2012. Much loved son, brother and husband*, I stopped and sank to my knees. The hard ground bit my flesh, but I didn't bother to shift. What was one more stab of pain?

"Hey, Matt. Your mum's been here, I see. Your flowers are fresh. She's good to you."

A pang of guilt went through me. I was neglectful of his grave and I was sure his parents complained about me to their friends, but what could I do? I just didn't see how offering flowers to a buried urn of ashes helped. Never had seen the point in it.

"I'm moving," I said, plucking a few dandelions from the grass that covered his plot. "To Northampton. I hope you don't think I'm mad or are cross at me for doing this, but you see, I've met someone." I paused and closed my eyes. "It's not what you think, not at all. I haven't met someone romantically. I met the man who has your heart and lungs. His name is Ruben Strong and he's friendly and polite and funny and saved me from the Blitz and a peacock." I smiled. "That probably sounds nuts, but it's true. He's asked me out for a drink—not a date—just to show me Northampton. There's lots to learn when you move to a new place. Remember what it was like when your parents moved up here from Devon? It took ages for them to find their way about, didn't it?"

I opened my eyes and glanced around. The cemetery was still and empty. I couldn't see another soul. "I haven't told him, though. Who I am or who you are. I don't think I should. That would be weird, wouldn't it? And besides, I shouldn't have gone looking for him. But then again, I could have by chance been in Northampton, wandering around the museum and suddenly bumped into him. That kind of thing happens all the time, right? Strangers meet."

Who was I kidding? I'd orchestrated it. Hell, I'd hired a private investigator to find him. It didn't get any more pre-meditated than that. But I really, truly hadn't meant to talk to him. That had never been my intention. I'd just wanted to look.

"So I'm not going to tell him…for now anyway. I'll just hang out with him for a bit. It makes it not so hard, like I'm with you, kind of. Oh, I know I'm not really. I'm not that far gone. A heart and lungs is only flesh and blood—a mechanical structure designed for sending blood and oxygen around the body. But…" I shook my head then readjusted my hat. "But he made me feel better—a bit better—and nothing has made me feel anything other than shit since that day. I could pretend that it has, but it hasn't." I sighed. "I miss you so much, Matt. If only we could turn back time. If only we'd done as you'd suggested that morning and both rang in sick and spent the day in bed, making love, drinking tea, dreaming of our future. If only…"

What was the point in if onlys? A tear slipped down my cheek and landed on my bare thigh, just missing the hem of my shorts. I rubbed it into my tanned skin.

"So I should go now and see if this is the right decision. I think it is. I hope it is. Either way giving it my best shot. What choice do I have? Oh, I know there is always a choice. I could curl up in a ball and let the world pass me by, pray that my life slips quickly to the end so we can be together again. To be honest, that sounds like the easiest option. But I'm taking the other path. I'm going to start fresh, be Katie, 'the new girl', and see how it fits, just for a few months. If I hate it, I'll come back to Leicester—no big deal."

I wiped my hand over his name, feeling the indent in the masonry. It was sharp and made my fingertips a little sore. Standing then, I brushed grass from my knees that were marked by the dry earth.

"I'll come back," I said. "Tell you how he's doing, so you know that the decision I made back then was right."

* * * *

"So why do people make a song and dance about moving house?" I asked myself four hours later as I put my hands on my hips and looked around my new flat.

In the bedroom, my clothes were hanging in the wardrobe and the bed had my covers on it. The soft fudge-colored sofa held my bright, citrus-hued cushions, and a picture of Spanish dancers—a wedding present—hung on the wall. My laptop was in the corner, on a small table with a comfy chair in front of it, and my new, compact kitchen was ready for use. Even the fridge held the basics from a convenient M&S on the next street.

There was a set of three shelves in a small dining area with a low window, and I'd set photographs on them—the one of our wedding day taking center place. Maybe it was time for him to move from the bedroom. I'd try it and see.

I sighed and flopped onto the couch, stared at the curtains I'd inherited. The same color as the sofa but with flecks of yellow in them. They were unusual and pretty and matched the colors I'd brought into the room, particularly the tall statue of a woman in a long dress that I'd placed on the windowsill. Yes, it looked nice. In fact, it more than looked nice. It *felt* nice. Felt right.

The window was open, letting in a slight breeze. I could hear children in the distance, playing in the park. A few minutes ago an ice-cream van had sung its way past. Those children were no doubt racing to get themselves a sweet treat.

It occurred to me that I felt a little lighter than usual. That damn weight in my stomach was still there, but maybe a tiny bit of it had been removed or chipped away—or something. The weight had shifted. That was for sure.

Yes, this had been the right thing to do—my new start—and I had to embrace my positivity.

I reached into my handbag and slid Ruben's card from the side pocket where I'd carefully stored it. I should call him now. See if he was free tonight to go for that drink. It would be a good end to what had turned out to be a good day.

Quickly, I checked the signal on my mobile then tapped in his number.

He answered on the third ring. "Hello?"

"Ruben?"

"Yes."

"Hi, this is Katie. We, er... We met at the museum last Saturday."

Oh, God, what will I do if he doesn't remember me?

Perhaps he had a string of girls and gave his number out to so many he'd never be able to recall which one I was.

"Ah, Katie, yes, of course I remember. How are you?"

Oh, thank goodness.

The wild fluttering in my chest settled—a fraction. "I'm okay, thanks. Just wondered if you were still up for going out, you know, for that drink."

"Absolutely. I'd love to. How about tonight?"

I could almost picture him smiling as he spoke. I smiled too. "Perfect. I'm not doing anything."

"Me neither, shall I pick you up?"

"Or we could meet. I noticed there's a bar attached to Mem-Saab. That's around the corner from me."

He laughed. "Corkers. Oh the champagne bar, oh what have I let myself in for? A woman with expensive taste."

"No, no, it's not like that. It's just... Well, it's the only one I've really noticed. We'll go somewhere else if you'd rather."

"Not at all, Corkers is the ideal progression from tea and cake in the park. Shall we say about eight?"

"Okay."

"They usually have piano music on a Saturday night. Is that all right with you?"

"Makes a change from the brass band."

"Certainly does."

There was a short silence. I broke it. "I'll see you later then."

"Yes, and, Katie…"

"Yes?"

"Thanks for calling. I was really hoping you would."

Chapter Five

The champagne bar, Corkers, was elegant and stylish. It appeared to be housed in an old school, and the inside was contemporary and chic — all walnut panels and cream leather. Ruben had been right. There was a grand piano someone was playing, a lazy jazz tune that tinkled around the soft furniture and up into the high-beamed ceiling.

I couldn't see Ruben when I stepped in and the place was fairly empty, so I knew I hadn't missed him. I walked up to the bar, my heels clacking on the floor, and ordered a glass of white wine, hoping he wouldn't be too long.

"Pinot grigio or sauvignon blanc?" the barman asked.

"Sauvignon, please."

"Hold the wine. We'll have champagne. Moët please."

I turned at the sound of Ruben's voice.

He smiled. "I was walking on the other side of the street. I called, but you didn't hear me."

"Oh, sorry," I said, smiling. "Hi."

His hair was freshly brushed, perhaps a little damp from a shower, and his jawline was clean-shaven. He smelled divine, an unusual scent that was woody but also fruity—berries maybe. It swirled around me, into my nose, and settled on my tongue. It was the first time I'd noticed the scent of another man in years.

"A bottle or two glasses, sir?"

"Have you eaten?" Ruben asked me.

"Yes." That was my standard answer whether I had or not, but actually, tonight it was true. I'd had a microwave meal an hour or so ago.

"We'll have a bottle. We'll be staying a while," Ruben said.

"Very good." The barman gestured to a corner spot that held a soft sofa and a low table. "I'll bring it straight over."

We moved to our seat.

"That was extravagant," I said.

"It's not often I have the company of a beautiful woman on a Saturday night," he said with a smile. "And you do look gorgeous."

"What, this old thing?" I plucked at the silky red blouse I'd teamed with skinny black jeans and red heels.

"Well, if that's your idea of a tatty old thing, I look forward to seeing your definition of something foxy."

"Foxy? You've spent too much time around those stuffed animals."

"You're probably right." He grinned and groaned at the same time. "I've got myself lost in another century."

He sat, and instead of sitting opposite, I settled next to him, twisted slightly and crossed my legs.

"Has the museum been busy this week?" I asked.

Ruben rested his arm along the back of the sofa, but we were sitting too far apart for it to be around me. I studied his legs, the stretch of his arms. He was tall and long-limbed. Matt had been the same, but much thicker set — his biceps had bulged when he'd worn a T-shirt, and his chest and shoulder muscles had rippled through a shirt on the occasions he'd worn one. Ruben was slighter. Whether he'd always been that way, I didn't know. Maybe he'd lost muscle mass since his illness. That wasn't to say he was skinny, just not beefy, the way Matt had been.

"Not particularly busy. I got those Earl Spencer pictures framed and up. Perhaps you'd like to come and see them sometime?"

"Yes, that would be nice."

"He was actually a pretty good artist."

The barman approached us. We sat in silence as he expertly popped the cork and poured two bubbling glasses of champagne. He then set the bottle in a silver ice bucket alongside several small bowls containing nuts, olives and triangular crisps.

"Cheers," Ruben said, handing me a glass. "Here's to your new life in Northampton.

It was the perfect toast — maybe a little too perfect — and I snatched in a breath, held it for a moment, willing myself to stay calm. I could do this. The decision had been made, and I wouldn't wobble on my tightrope. "To Northampton." I touched the rim of my glass to his then drank.

He did the same. "Mmm," he said. "I don't normally drink, so I might as well enjoy the good stuff when I do."

"That makes sense." I wondered if it was because of the transplant that he didn't drink. I knew he'd be on tablets to stop his body rejecting Matt's organs. He'd have to take them for the rest of his life. Was he allowed to drink alcohol?

"Has your work been busy?" he asked.

"No, not really. Christmas is our chaotic time, and then January when the sales are on. People are pretty minimalist on makeup this time of year, especially in this heat."

He looked at me and smiled. I wondered if he was examining my makeup. I had only a sweep of powder, slick of mascara and the barest hint of tinted gloss. This wasn't a date, after all. Just a drink.

I again sipped my champagne.

"So, um, how long have you been widowed?" he asked.

His question surprised me. I'd thought we were just swapping pleasantries. "Oh, er...nearly two years."

His brow creased. "I'm sorry. I was thinking about you after we met in the park last week. How young you are to have gone through losing your husband."

"I'm twenty-seven. Matt was a bit older than me." I paused, wondering again if my husband's name would mean anything to Ruben. But his concerned expression didn't falter. Of course, Matt's name wouldn't mean anything. He had his heart and lungs, but he didn't know his name. They wouldn't have told him that. It was against the rules.

I sighed. "He was thirty when he had an accident at work."

Ruben sipped his champagne. The glass pressed on his bottom lip, flattening it slightly. When he'd finished, he placed the drink on the table and sat back again, tipping his head as if urging me to continue.

"He worked on a construction site. Scaffolding was his responsibility," I went on. "He was in charge of a team of apprentices. Something went wrong. The inquest went into details but basically someone hadn't fixed about a two dozen poles together that should have been joined and the whole thing collapsed. Matt fell with it, not very far really. He could have walked away they said, without even a broken bone, but his safety hat, it was faulty… He died instantly when a pole landed on his head from about thirty feet up." I tucked my hair behind my ears and touched my lips, remembering that awful day and the decision I'd had to make about his organs going for donation. Only his brain had died in the accident. The rest of him had lived on for a few hours with the help of a ventilator, making him a suitable donor, and part of him was still living on now, in Ruben, not three feet away from me.

Ruben said nothing. He gave me a sad smile, and his dark gaze connected with mine. I got the feeling he understood pain Maybe not my pain, but certainly the terror of death, the shadow that lurked close. It always amazed me that so many people treated death like an unsubstantiated rumor, when you only had to look around to see the facts.

"It was horrendous," I said. "The worst time of my life. We'd been married for three years, together for five. We had all kinds of plans and then suddenly it was over. He was gone. Not a goodbye, not a farewell hug, nothing. Gone. He just wasn't there anymore." My eyes filled. I could see the tears brimming on my lower lids. I blinked, hoping they'd reabsorb, but overspill point had been reached.

Ruben stretched over and laid his warm hand on mine. "I'm sorry. I shouldn't have asked."

"It's okay, asking or not asking doesn't change the facts." I caught the single tear and the bizarre thought that, *Thank goodness this isn't a date*, crossed my mind. If it was, it would be bloody disastrous. Ten minutes in and I was crying. "I miss him, of course, but I'm trying to get on with my life. I think Northampton will help, when I settle in. It will give me the change I need."

"And you can start making new memories," he said gently. "That's the thing about change. Everything feels empty to start with, but then when you settle into it—over days, weeks, months—that change becomes the norm and it's not different anymore. You find your feet and a new way to be—a new place for you in the world that feels right." He paused and rubbed his chest, pressing his black, short-sleeved shirt against his sternum. "I think you're brave to have moved away from Leicester. It must be hard when your people are there."

"My parents are in Yorkshire. It's just friends I've left." I sighed and pulled my hand from his, reached for my drink. "But I feel like I've left him, even though he's not there really. Well, unless you count Hill Rise cemetery."

"Do you go there often?"

"No, but I went today."

He raised his eyebrows. "You did?"

"Yes, I had things to tell him. Well, to get off my chest anyway. Usually I leave his mother to deal with his grave. I think she likes it."

Ruben inclined his head, as though understanding what I meant.

"So tell me." I pasted on my I'm-okay-now smile. "What else is there around here for me to see?"

Ruben blinked slowly then nodded, ever so slightly, as if he could see straight through my carefully applied mask and knew damn well I'd changed the subject on purpose. "Well, next month there's the hot-air balloon festival, right there." He gestured out of the window. "If your new place faces the park, you'll have a great view. You won't need to buy a ticket. My flat is like a front-row seat."

"Oh, that sounds nice."

He grinned. "It's good fun. They have a bizarre assortment of balloons, all shapes and sizes—some like giant, sweet monsters, others shaped like houses or fish. It gets international coverage."

"I'll look out for that. And what about these country pubs you mentioned?"

"More than you can shake a stick at, though one of my favorites is The Fox and Hound in Great Brington. A really pretty thatched-cottage affair, it has beautiful gardens in the summer and roaring log fires in the winter and the food is delicious."

"Sounds lovely."

"It is. Maybe if you put something less tatty on, I could take you there."

I laughed. "Cheeky bugger."

He laughed too, a genuine chuckle, the way mine had been. I touched my lips, feeling the air from my giggle. It had just bubbled up, popped out. It had been wonderfully effortless and reminded me of a time when laughs had been ten a penny.

The bar began to fill—glamorous women, stylish men, all enjoying a drink and nice music in chilled-out surroundings. I felt relaxed, and I think Ruben did too. We chatted about the museum and Northampton. He told me about his parents who lived nearby and were golf enthusiasts. He also told me about his brother and his wife who lived in London and had twin girls.

When the champagne bottle was empty, I excused myself and went to the restroom. After slipping out of the cubicle and freshening up, I looked at myself in the mirror.

A Katie I hadn't seen in a long time stared back at me. I was out, on a Saturday night, my chestnut-colored hair was tonged. I wore makeup and my blouse was undone to reveal just a little bit of chest — not that I had much cleavage these days.

Two girls, early twenties, burst into the restroom. The sound of the piano increased for the few seconds the door was open and carried in on a wave of conversation.

"He's gorgeous," one said to the other, flicking her hair over her shoulders. "I'm so glad you set me up with Ian. Just my type."

Her friend grinned. "I knew you'd get on. You have so much in common, and next week we're going to Yarmouth. Come with us. It'll be a laugh."

"Really?"

"Yes."

They took no notice of me and carried on with chatter about their men. I watched as the one with the new fella brushed her hair, added a spritz of perfume to her wrist and neck then rolled up a bright pink lipstick.

"Never thought I'd date a fireman," she said. "I owe you big time, Cheryl."

"He's as into you as you are him. I've known Ian ages. I can tell when he likes what he sees."

"Do you think so?"

"Yeah, absolutely. Come on. Let's get back out there. You've got some serious flirting to do."

They barged out in a tangle of giggles and linked arms.

How wonderful to be so carefree, so optimistic about the future, so enamored by a new man.

I thought of Ruben waiting for me in the bar. If this had been a date, would I be all excited and giggly? Counting my lucky stars for having found someone so gorgeous?

After retrieving my lip gloss from the bottom of my bag, I applied a delicate swipe. Ruben was a great-looking bloke. There was no doubt about that. I wondered why he didn't have a girlfriend, or why he'd been free on a Saturday night. It wasn't as if he was still sick. He had a new heart and lungs, he was getting on with his life, he could return to the land of the living and be strong, as his name suggested. Not that he'd told me anything about his illness or operation all evening. I didn't know if he was purposefully not mentioning it or if it just wasn't a big deal for him anymore.

How could it not be?

I dropped my gloss away, smoothed my hair then checked my teeth for crisp fragments. It was probably time to go home. It was getting late and this would be my first night in my new flat.

Ruben smiled at me as I walked toward him. "Would you like to go somewhere else or stay here and have another drink?" he asked.

"I think I'll go home, if you don't mind."

"Whatever you want." He stood, straightened his shirt and checked the sofa to make sure we hadn't left anything. But in this hot weather, jackets were redundant, even in the evening.

We wound our way through the bar, and I spotted the two girls who'd been in the restroom. They were sitting at a table with two handsome men, all had smiles on their faces, all seemed oblivious to the room. It was just them, out, having fun. They had their whole future ahead of them. They had history to make.

A pang of jealousy hit me. I wanted that carefree, self-absorbedness again—a life without that damn anvil weighing me down.

Ruben slipped his hand to the small of my back, steered me around a group of four men holding pints and chattering loudly. For a moment that weight lifted, as if he were holding some of the load for me. Once outside he dropped his hand from me. I took a deep breath and tried to keep that light feeling inside.

"It still smells hot," I said, holding the railing and walking down the four steps to the path.

"I love that smell," he said, "tarmac and ice cream."

"Sun lotion and grass," I added.

"Yeah, definitely grass. I guess that's the park smell." He gestured left then right. "Which way are you from here?"

"Down past Darren Street."

"Okay. I'll walk you."

"I'll be fine, really."

He huffed and folded his arms. "What kind of man do you think I am?"

I smiled. "I'm sensing stubborn."

"Got it in one."

We started walking.

"My father would tan my hide if I let a girl go home on her own after we'd been out on a date," he said

"A date?" The word caught in my mouth.

"Well, you know…a drink."

"Have we been on a date?" I felt a little woozy from the champagne, but not enough that I couldn't think straight.

"I don't know. I guess some people might think so, but we can just call it a drink if you want." He paused. "I'm sorry. Have I said something wrong?"

"No. No, I don't think so." I rubbed my forehead. I'd told Matt earlier, at his graveside, that I wasn't going on a date with Ruben, but I had. The definition of a date was two people going out and getting to know each other. That was exactly what Ruben and I had done.

"Katie, I'm sorry. Look. I've had a really nice time tonight. I think you're great, gorgeous, but if you just want to be friends, I get that. No pressure, seriously, and no dates if that's not your thing either."

Dates not my thing? I didn't really know. It had been so long. "I've enjoyed myself, Ruben. It's just…"

"Katie." He stopped walking, reached out and rested his hand on my shoulder.

I paused and looked up at him. I liked the weight of his hand on me, the same as when he'd pressed it into the small of my back a few minutes ago. Physical connection with Ruben suited me. It made me feel nice, safe.

"You haven't dated since Matt died, have you?"

I let out a huge breath I hadn't even realized I'd been holding. "No." I touched my wedding ring, spun it the way I often did when nervous. "It's hard not to feel unfaithful to him."

"I can see how you'd feel like that."

"Can you?"

He nodded. "Yes. It's not like you're divorced, is it? You still love him."

I swallowed. Steadied myself on the tightrope. "I'll always love him, but I've made a decision, lately, to get on with my life. His is over, but mine isn't. I have to move on."

He slid his hand down my arm. When he reached my bare elbow, his skin was soft on mine. "Moving on isn't easy, but I'm happy to help if I can."

"You have, already — more than you know."

He smiled and gently took my hand in his. "Come on. Let's get you home."

We walked in silence. I concentrated on the feel of his fingers, the heat of his palm and the way our forearms brushed a few times. We fit together, in a strange, messed-up-jigsaw kind of a way. Ruben and I, we clicked.

"This is me," I said, stopping as we reached the stone steps that led up to my flat.

"Nice spot," he said with an approving nod.

"Would you — ?"

"Can I — ?"

We both spoke at the same time then grinned.

"You go first," I said.

"Sure?"

"Yes."

"Okay," he said, "would you like to go for a picnic tomorrow? There's a reservoir nearby, Pitsford. We could go later in the day, when it's not so hot. Only if you fancy it. Doesn't matter if you're busy or something. Whatever, really… Just thought you might like it…"

I looked up at my flat. The lounge window was in darkness. I had absolutely nothing to do tomorrow and knew no one but Ruben in this town of museums, champagne bars and hot-air balloons. "That sounds nice."

He smiled. "It's just a picnic — no pressure, no date presumptions."

"You're very sweet. You know that?"

"Oh, no." He groaned. "Not the *sweet* word. Can't I be tough and manly — or maybe even tall, dark and handsome?"

"You fit into the tall, dark and handsome category," I said with a smile then suddenly felt shy and silly. I looked at my feet, took my hand from his.

He laughed. "Did you forget to put your contact lenses in?"

"I don't wear them." I giggled again. Ruben had a way of diffusing my emotions. He'd done it all evening. Whatever I'd said, it had just worked out all right.

"So, shall I pick you up about five?" he asked.

"Perfect."

A purple sports car purred past. It caught Ruben's attention, and he followed it with his gaze until it went out of view.

"You like that car?" I asked.

"Yeah, it's okay."

"You mentioned Silverstone when we were at the park," I said, studying the way the orange glow from a street lamp above cast the angles of his face in shadow. "Working with Formula One."

"I did indeed say that."

He pushed his fingers through his hair. Several strands stayed sticking up wonky. I had a sudden urge to flatten them down, see what his hair would feel like. Matt had always kept his hair super-short. It had almost been sharp when I'd run my hand up it the wrong way. Ruben's, however, looked soft and silky, as if it would fill my fingers, flow around my knuckles.

"So are you going to tell me about it?" I asked. "This fancy job."

He shrugged. "Tomorrow."

"Okay." The no pressure thing could work both ways. "Five o'clock, you said?"

"Yes."

"What shall I bring?"

"Just yourself."

Chapter Six

I was hot and weary. We'd walked almost halfway around the huge reservoir. It was more of a meander, really, because the sun was still strong, despite the fact it was early evening Ruben carried a rucksack on his back, and I had a blue blanket beneath my arm rolled up like a sausage.

"We should stop and eat soon. Save you carrying all of that stuff," I said. "What have you got in there anyway?"

"Ah, now that's for me to know and you to find out." He tapped the side of his nose.

I laughed. "Man of mystery."

"Mystery is better than sweet, I suppose." He grinned and pointed. "How about over there, away from the path?"

It was a nice spot by a copse of silver birches. The grass was long and pale, the slight breeze whispering through it in waves.

"Suits me."

We left the path, and the soft blades of grass tickled my legs. When we reached the spot Ruben had suggested, I spied a better one, over the next mound.

"Is over there nicer?" I asked. "It has some dappled shade."

"Looks good."

After another short stomp, I spread out the blanket. The long grass was holding it up a little, as if it were on springy bubbles. I sat and tapped it down, trying to flatten it.

Ruben patted it, too, then slipped the bag from his back and set it to one side.

"Oh, it's good to be off my feet," I said, stretching my legs out in front of me. I was wearing denim shorts, soft canvas shoes and a white T-shirt teamed with a pale blue silk scarf.

"I'm sorry. Have I worn you out?" He sat next to me.

"Everything is an effort when it's hot. Don't you think?"

"Yes, it's even hard to breathe." His gaze caught mine then he looked away, busied himself with the bag. "So, we have chicken skewers, cucumber sandwiches, sausages…" He was pulling out plastic containers. "And crisps and carrot sticks and dips. Also hard-boiled eggs."

"Hard-boiled eggs?" I said with an amused grin.

He held up one. It looked small in his big fingers. "What's wrong with hard-boiled eggs?"

"Nothing, it's just funny that you brought them."

He smiled and shrugged. "I like them. But I'm afraid there's no cheese. I hate cheese." He pulled his mouth downwards and shuddered. "Can't even bear it in the house these days."

"That's okay. I'm used to not eating cheese, and it looks like there's plenty to keep us going." I snagged a cucumber sandwich, and he passed me a can of Coke. "Thanks."

Ruben set the egg down and started on some chicken.

"You can't see the path from here," I said, nodding in the direction we'd come.

"No, nor the water."

"I've admired the reservoir plenty." I sipped my drink. "It's nice to find a quiet spot."

"I didn't come to admire the reservoir view anyway," he said with shrug.

"What do you mean?"

He set his dark gaze on me. "I have the perfect view right here."

I resisted the urge to check my clothing and fuss with my hair as I felt heat prickle its way up my neck to my cheeks. "Thanks, I think."

He smiled and dipped his hand into the bag.

Much as my cheeks had no doubt flared, his were stained a little red too.

I finished my sandwich and reached for a carrot stick, dipped it in a pot of hummus.

What were we like, the pair of us? We were both messed up, both misfits, both been dealt a really shitty hand in life. Though, of course, he didn't know I knew that about him—that his cards just hadn't added up. Maybe it was time to get that onto the table.

"So tell me," I said, crunching my carrot and doing my best to act casual, "what made you stop changing Formula One tires in fifteen seconds? Isn't that what you said at the café? Fifteen seconds?"

He popped a crisp into his mouth then flicked a tiny black bug from his gray T-shirt. "Yeah, sometimes quicker."

"Big career change—Silverstone to the museum."

He must have been asked the question before. In fact, he'd seemed surprised that first day I'd met him when I hadn't probed further. It was a bit like my wedding ring question, I supposed—one that kept being innocently asked by near strangers.

But was I a near stranger? Or had Ruben and I moved on to friendship? I liked to think so.

He took a deep breath, as though steeling himself. "I got ill. I couldn't work for a few years. It knocked my career in Formula One on the head."

I nodded, took a sip of my Coke.

"I had a heart condition—bummer really. It came on quick, messed me up big time. I had to stop work." He hesitated, glanced at the birches wending in the breeze. "To start with, the doctors thought they'd be able to control the cardiomyopathy—that's what it was called—with drugs, but soon it became apparent that wasn't going to work." He shrugged. "Not if I was going to have any quality of life anyway."

"So how did you get this, er…cardiomyopathy? Was it something you did? Something you caught?"

"No, just bloody bad luck. It can run in families, but no one else in mine has it."

"And it made you really, really sick?"

"Yes."

"How sick? What couldn't you do because of your bad heart?" Perhaps I'd sounded hard, but I needed to know, had to understand why he'd needed a new one so desperately.

He sighed. "Where do you want me to start?"

"From the beginning."

"Okay, to begin with I was just a bit short of breath, my ankles were swelling, I was tired, had headaches. I felt like an old man, even though I was young and fit. So I went to the doctor, thinking he'd say I was working too hard—or maybe I'd picked something up from when we'd been abroad racing. He sent me straight into hospital for tests and within a day, my world had turned upside down."

"I know what that's like."

He leaned forward, rested his index finger on my wedding band. "I'm sure you do."

I pressed my lips together as a sudden vision of Matt, myself and Ruben all standing in a triangle, holding hands, hit me.

"It became apparent," he said, pulling me from that image, "pretty quickly that the drugs weren't working. Even on high doses, I could hardly breathe. It was like sucking in air through a wet rag most of the time. My damn floppy-muscled heart just couldn't get the oxygen around my body. Working was impossible. Then going out became too much. I moved back in with my parents. It took me all of my time to get out of bed, dressed and walk to the living room each day. I'd sleep then, after Mum brought my breakfast and a mountain of pills, often until mid-afternoon. I was quite literally slipping away."

"That's awful." I looked at him now, slim, tanned and with a sparkle in his eye. I couldn't imagine him being so wrecked.

"Awful is the word, but without my parents, those four years would have been so much worse. They were my rock."

"You didn't have a girlfriend or anything?"

"No. I'd been traveling a lot, with the team. We'd just come back from Monaco. Had a blast." He smiled, looked wistful. "I was living the dream, flying high. There wasn't one special woman in my life. Will you hate me for saying I was just having fun with *lots* of special women?"

I smiled. "Nothing wrong with having fun. I used to have lots of fun too. I like fun."

He caught my gaze then glanced away, put the lid on the tub of sandwiches to deter a tiny fly. "I was put on the list pretty quickly, but they manage your expectations so you feel like it will never happen. Then if it does…" He lifted his hands, raised his eyes heavenward. "You feel honored."

"What list? Like what will never happen?" Of course I knew.

He dropped his hands to his lap and looked at me, his gaze boring deep into mine, penetrating to my core.

"What list?" I asked again, needing Ruben to tell me. Desperate for him to say he had a new heart, a heart that had belonged to a person who was good and kind and had given him back his life. Changed him from that ruined shell into a vibrant, handsome man again who was now enjoying a picnic in the sunshine with a girl.

Still he said nothing—instead, he curled his fingers beneath his T-shirt and began to peel it off.

I studied his belly, slender with a dark trail of hair rising from the waistband of his jeans. A little higher and his navel was revealed, the hair here sparser and fanned to the sides. Another few inches higher and set in the very center of his torso was the base of a smooth pink scar. As Ruben lifted his T-shirt up and off, it continued right over his sternum, to just beneath the hollow of his throat.

He tossed the T-shirt aside and looked down at his chest. It was sprinkled with hairs, but none on the scar. That was flat and pale, probably a couple of finger-widths wide.

I stared, too, knowing that beneath that scar was Matt's beating heart. Through that wound Matt's heart had been gently passed, filling the space of an old, defunct heart that was no longer up to the job. Surgeons had carefully joined arteries and veins, made one working, functioning body out of scraps. It was Ruben who'd got possession of the sum total.

I moved onto my knees, sitting the same way Ruben was, and pressed my palm over his chest.

He sucked in a breath and placed his hand over mine.

"You were on the transplant list," I whispered. "You have a new heart."

"Yes."

"You were dying."

He nodded. "Yes, I was."

His skin was warm, and his hairs tickled my fingertips. The *thud-thud-thud* of Matt's heart vibrated through my palm. "A new heart was the only thing that could save you, wasn't it?"

"Yes. I didn't really need the lungs, but they say it's easier to move them as a package—something to do with all the blood vessels."

I nodded. I'd heard that too. "What does it feel like? To have a part of someone else inside you?"

"Gratitude is the strongest emotion, the fact that a grieving family made such an amazingly difficult decision on the worst day of their lives to benefit a stranger. The gratitude is scarily consuming at times." He paused. "One day, soon I hope, I'll say thank you in a letter or perhaps face-to-face. My coordinator says that can happen when I'm ready. But words just seem so inadequate, not enough to express my appreciation. I wish there was something I could do for them in return. I need to work on those thoughts a bit more before I can put pen to paper."

I bit my bottom lip. Put all my concentration into balancing. I needed to hear the rest of this. "Go on. What else do you feel?"

"There's relief. I'm not dying anymore, but there's still fear. My body is constantly trying to reject what's good for it, and then there's the absolute determination to just be normal and move on." He shrugged. "Move into my new way of being, anyway. Can't be quite the dare-devil, adrenaline junkie I once was. Well, not for a few more years at least." He gave a half smile.

"Well you have to look after it." I nodded at his chest. "That heart."

"Yes, I intend to, but, Katie, I understand if you don't want to…" He looked away.

"What?"

He turned back to me, shook his head. "I'm as out of the whole dating game as you are. I've just found myself a quiet job in a quiet place and I'm happy to be alive. I haven't been looking for romance or love, only trying to put the pieces back together. You might not want to be around someone like me."

As he'd spoken, his sweet, cola-laced breath had washed over my face. I breathed it in. This was air that had been inhaled and exhaled through Matt's lungs.

Matt's lungs.

I breathed deeper, breathing him in, allowing that air to fill my chest, circulate my body—air from lungs that I had gasped and panted with in a hundred beautiful memories.

A full-body tingle attacked me. My eyes stung, but I fought for control. Maintained it, just. "You're alive," I whispered, not wanting to move my hand from his chest. Feeling Matt's heart beating was like coming home. How many nights had I gone to sleep listening to that rhythmic sound?

"I'm alive." He softened his voice. "And so are you."

I nodded. "Yes."

"So?" He used his other hand to tilt my chin, bring my attention to his face.

"What?" I whispered.

He paused, worried at his bottom lip with his teeth. "Can you cope with a broken man?"

"You're not broken. You're fixed." I bit back a sob that was threatening to erupt. "You have a wonderful new heart that feels perfect and strong, like it will beat forever. You're not broken anymore, Ruben. You're fixed. They made you better."

He frowned. His eyes were moist too. "I hated being broken."

"Me too." I let a tear overspill, unconcerned by its track down my cheek.

Without a doubt, the decision I'd made when I'd sat in intensive care, holding Matt's lifeless hand, with the organ-retrieval team waiting for my answer, had been the right one. It had been painful, torturous and as Ruben had just said, the worst day of my life, but it had been the only thing that had made sense.

He caught the tear with the pad of his thumb. "Don't cry."

"I'm sorry. I'm just happy for you. You've been through hell. And I know what a horrible place that is."

"Right now it feels like I'm in heaven." He smiled. "I can almost hear harps."

A slightly hysterical little giggle burst from me, then I did what I'd been wanting to do all evening. I slipped my fingers into his soft hair, cradled his skull, and pressed my lips to his.

Chapter Seven

"Katie," he whispered when I pulled back from our soft kiss.

"I'm sorry." I could taste him, just a little. It hadn't been a big, open-mouthed snog, merely a touch. But still, it had spoken a thousand words, and it was the first time I'd kissed anyone other than Matt in years.

"No. Please don't apologize." He placed his hands on my shoulders, his thumbs grazing my collarbones through my T-shirt. "I liked it, but...are you sure?"

"I'm trying to put my life back together, too, Ruben. Matt will always be with me. No one can replace him." I paused, juddered in a breath and put my hand on Ruben's chest again. "Our time together was cut short, but the memories I have... They're good memories." I tried to find the right words—my emotions were tangled, my thoughts jumbled—but basically I just wanted to be with Ruben. It felt right. In a very basic, limbic part of my brain, Ruben was someone I needed. "But I want to make new memories, happy ones, fun ones. I can't be a sad widow who everyone feels sorry for anymore. It's not what Matt would have wanted for me, I know that."

"If he loved you, he would have wanted you to find happiness again." He stroked his thumbs to the base of my throat, shifting my silky scarf. It was a small, delicate caress that sent a shiver of something scarily like desire tickling over my skin.

"He did love me," I said, "with all of his heart." And did that heart still love me? The one I could feel beating right now? Is that where love was stored, in the fibers of the cardiac muscle? And if so, did that mean Matt's love had been transferred into Ruben when Matt's heart was transplanted? Did Ruben love me already, because of the reassignment of an organ?

"Katie?" He frowned a little.

"For the first time, it feels right to hear that said."

"What?"

"That he would have wanted me to be happy. Oh, it's been said to me by lots of well-meaning friends over the last year, since the anniversary of his death, and I've just nodded and agreed, put on my usual fake smile." I shook my head. "But now, here... Yes, he would have wanted me to be looking for happiness again, and I want to find it—not because it's what I'm supposed to be doing, but because it's what I want. I need to feel alive again, because—like you said—I am alive."

Ruben smiled, the edges of his mouth tilting a fraction and the creases at the corners of his eyes deepening. "Me too. God, me too." He kissed me, a gentle connection, his tongue dipping into my mouth the tiniest amount.

I slid both my hands over his shoulders. He wrapped his arms around my body, and our chests touched. My breasts, through my top, squeezed up against his firm pectoral muscles.

His kiss was tender and sweet, his lips a new shape for me to learn. I touched the tip of my tongue to his, drew in the slightly salty, masculine flavor of him and knew it was something I wanted more of.

He pulled me closer still. I shifted and next thing I knew he was resting me backwards. I unfolded my legs, stretched out and knocked away the pot of carrot sticks.

The feel of Ruben over me, kissing me, was exciting, frightening, wonderful and painful all at the same time.

He kissed across my cheek, to my ear. His breaths were loud and he held his weight carefully on his elbows. I ran my hands down his smooth back, tracing the slopes and rises of his spine then over the planes of his shoulder blades, all the time staring up at the cloudless sky and the bows of the birches, their tiny leaves shivering in the breeze.

"You smell like flowers," he whispered into the shell of my ear.

"I do?"

"Yes, so pretty." He lifted his head and looked down at me. "Kissing you here...now... It's my top new memory."

I smiled. The smile grew and grew until it balled my cheeks and another giggle escaped. "I think it's mine too."

He kissed me again. I shut my eyes, lost myself in the moment. That small shiver of desire was back. The need for more—skin-on-skin and to get closer—was growing. Ruben had that certain something that worked for me. His smell, taste and the way he made me feel as if everything would be all right... It was something I could get hooked on.

I ran my hands over the waistband of his jeans, stroked his arse cheeks through the denim. Damn, what a cute bum. Taut and the perfect handful.

He dropped his weight a little more, our chests pressed harder together and his groin pushed into my right hip. He deepened the kiss and a fizz of lust sparked through me. It couldn't be ignored. My nipples were tight. There was a tug in my lower abdomen, the start of a need — a need I hadn't thought of for so long.

I lifted my left leg, curled it over the back of his and squeezed up against him. It was then I felt a long, hard bulge.

"Ruben," I gasped into his mouth as a fist of something raw and primitive gripped me. *Could we? Here?*

"Damn, I'm sorry, I..." He lifted up, completely off me.

"What's the matter?"

He lay at my side, head propped on his hand. He wore a pained expression. "I'm sorry," he said again.

"It's okay," I said, touching his cheek and squashing that first flame of lust that had a hold of me — a lust that since becoming a widow had been absent in my life.

"No, I'm sorry. That's too much for you. Too fast. I'm so sorry."

"Ruben, shh, I was enjoying it too." I stroked his face, adoring the slightly scratchy feel of his stubbled jawline. "You're a hot bloke. Why wouldn't I?"

He huffed. "That's kind of you to say."

"Kind?"

"Yeah, kind, you know, with this." He looked at his scar. "And I used to be a bit more muscled, you know?"

"Really? You think that makes a difference to me? Your scar? How you used to be?"

"I don't know. You're a beautiful woman, Katie." He reached for a lock of my hair, twirled it in his fingers, studying how it coiled and hung there. "You could have any man you want."

"I don't want any man. I want someone who can make me smile but understands if I don't want to. I need someone who's been to the same dark places as me and gets what it's like to be starting over. For me, that acceptance is sexy and…" I hesitated then decided just to go for it. Impulsive always had been my middle name. "And so are you, Ruben. Really sexy."

His gaze caught mine. "Damn, I got lucky when you walked into the museum that day."

A small kernel of guilt popped inside me. I'd orchestrated our meeting, yet he thought it was coincidence.

He adjusted his position, grimaced slightly as he moved his hips.

"Are you okay?" I asked, pushing guilt into the locked box it belonged. I'd had enough negative emotions to last me forever. Guilt could bugger off and leave me alone.

"Yeah, fine. Well, I will be in a few minutes." He gave a wry grin. "Can't exactly do anything about it here, can we?"

I dropped my hand from his cheek to his chest, circled his taut, dark nipple. I was ready for some good feelings. "Maybe."

His smile fell. "Can we, er…take it slow. This, us?"

"Absolutely." I stilled my movements.

He frowned at my lock of hair hugging his finger, let it unwind then placed it on my shoulder. "It's not that I don't like you, that I'm not..." He paused. "Well, you know I'm turned on by you. You've just felt the evidence of that, but..."

I rested my hand on his arm, studied the cute little mole on his cheek. It was small and flat, perfectly round. "What is it, Ruben?"

He screwed up his eyes, wrinkled his nose.

"Tell me."

"Fuck," he said, staring at me. "It's been bloody years since I've done it and certainly not with this new heart. And I don't think public sex would do me any favors." He gave a nervous laugh. His cheeks were flushed. "The thrill of it might finish me off."

Something very deep inside me melted for Ruben. He'd clearly been having a wild time before his illness—chasing races and the dreams that went with them. But now here he was, picking up the pieces, adjusting to a slower world and a new way to be in it.

But he could do it. I was on that same path and managing to put one step in front of the other. It was beginning to make sense—this route—and I'd help Ruben on his way if he needed me to. I couldn't carry him—I wasn't that strong—but I could hold his hand. Let him follow me some of the way. Who knew? Maybe one day we'd both run, sprint and leap again.

"It's been a long time for me too," I said. "We'll go slow. I think we both need that."

He reached for my hand, lifted it from his arm and turned it over, palm up. "Thank you."

"You don't need to say thank you."

"I do. You've made me feel like a hot-blooded male again and I appreciate that, but even more I appreciate your understanding." He placed a gentle kiss in the center of my palm.

"For me there was only ever Matt. He was my first love, my only love."

He breathed deeply then let it out slowly. "In which case you are very lucky. *Matt* was very lucky."

"He was fond of saying that."

"I can see why." He paused, a new sparkle appearing in his eye. "I want to take you somewhere, somewhere really special to me, but it has to be tomorrow evening. Can you handle spending more time with me?"

"Of course. Where?"

"It's a surprise."

"That sounds intriguing."

"It's fun." He pulled a face. "Loud though."

"Oh, no, not the Blitz room again at the museum?" I smiled. "I can't cope with that."

"No, definitely not there."

* * * *

I looked at Skin Deep from across the pedestrianized street. The sign was the same—pale green with pink writing—and the promotional poster in the window identical to the one in Leicester. But this was a different shop, new people, new customers—all part of the new me.

I twirled my wedding band around and around in a fast, nervous gesture. What would I fiddle with when I wasn't wearing it? What would keep my fingers busy?

That morning when I'd been getting ready for my first day at Skin Deep Northampton, I'd had the sudden urge to take my ring off. I'd been eating toast and marmalade, staring at the news without watching, when the idea had rushed into my head all bloated with self-importance. Now I couldn't stop paying heed to it, toying with the possibility.

I stared at the ring. It was pale gold and the edges slightly beveled. I hadn't taken it off since the day we were married. When Matt had slipped it on my finger in front of God and our family and friends, I'd truly believed I would wear it until my dying day.

Yet here I was, standing on an unfamiliar road in an unfamiliar town, about to do the unthinkable. Remove it.

I spun it faster. It was a little big. It seemed my weight loss had even extended to my fingers. Maybe taking it off was for the best. It would only go missing now that it was so loose. If that happened, I'd be crushed. This ring was the symbol of Matt's love for me, my devotion to him, our promises to be true to each other for as long as we both lived.

Yet he didn't live.

I stopped rotating it, lifted my hand and kissed the band. "I'll always love you," I whispered before sliding it off. There was a slight dip in my finger, an indent. I rubbed it, liking the feeling. It was as if I was still wearing it, in a way.

Quickly, before I dropped the ring or changed my mind, I secured it in my purse, in a little zipped compartment. Maybe I'd find a chain to wear it on. Perhaps it would sit in my jewelry box. Whatever happened, I would always keep it. It would always be my most precious possession.

I took a deep breath, straightened my black blouse and checked the fly zip on my neat black trousers — standard uniform for Skin Deep — then stepped across the cobbles.

Now, when I met my Northampton colleagues, I would be 'Katie the new girl' or 'Katie from Leicester' or 'Katie with the long, brown hair'. 'Katie the widow' had to become a much smaller part of who I was. It was the only way I'd find the happiness I knew Matt would want for me. The happiness I wanted for myself.

* * * *

My first day flew by. The manageress, a Jamaican lady called Corine, who only just fit between the stands of products because her bottom was so wide, was lovely and welcoming. She smiled all day, flashing dazzling white teeth, and chatting about her life in the Caribbean. She had a daughter who lived there and was soon coming for a visit to England.

There was one more girl in the front of the shop with me—Janine. She was pretty and perfectly made up. She, too, was chatty, but mainly about her friends, the bloke she'd just split up with and the one she liked now. By the time mid-afternoon hit, I knew the history of her love life in great detail. It was nice—freeing in a way—not to have her hesitating about telling me saucy snippets, worrying that she might upset me or sound insensitive to my situation. I smiled and nodded, answered appropriately and enjoyed the light feeling her flow of conversation had given me. Not being thought of as a sad widow was liberating.

At five o'clock I was in the back room, checking in some new stock, when Corine called through from the front of shop in her smooth drawl, "Katie, chicken, there's a guy asking for you and he has got the cutest damn smile I have ever seen."

"Really?"

"Yeah." She poked her head around the door. "Get your toosh out here before I jump your man." She rolled her eyes and grinned. "Lucky thing, you."

I put down the box of organic lipstick and dashed through to the shop front.

Ruben stood there with hands in his pockets and his cheeks a little red. He looked big and dark amongst the dainty, pink girly stuff surrounding him.

"You can come and see us anytime," Corine saying to him. "And if you want me to help you sample any of our massage oils, just say the word." She cackled loudly.

Ruben shifted from one foot to the other. He appeared to clench his hands into fists in his pockets. "Thanks for the offer. Might just take you up on it." He smiled.

"Oh, you should do that." Corine held up her big, dark fingers and waggled them, the gold of her many rings catching in the light. "I could work magic on a body like yours with these hands."

I suppressed a giggle. She was outrageous, but it had all been said with a fun-soaked smile.

"Ruben." I stepped up to him. "Hi."

"Katie." He'd been holding his own with Corine but still, there was a flash of relief in his eyes that I'd arrived.

"What are you doing here?" Not that I was complaining. A twirl of pleasure had wound itself in my stomach. Damn, the bloke was cute. I could see why Corine was having fun with him.

"We said we'd go out this evening, remember? Mystery tour."

"Yes, but…" I glanced at my watch. "I have another half an hour to work."

"Oh, nonsense, chicken," Corine said. "You get yourself out there now." She waved at me then the open door to the street. "I don't think there's going to be a rush on Pebble Pink Lippy in the next half an hour. Go on out with your sexy man."

"But—"

"No buts." She shook her head, and the bun of wild black hair on the top of her head wobbled. "You've worked your little socks off today with that inventory and, to be honest, we're thrilled to have you. Been too much for just me and Janine. Your arrival is a godsend."

A warmth settled inside me. I'd had a good first day, positive all round, and to know that I was wanted, appreciated, was like the icing on the cake. So why did my eyes feel tingly? Like tears wanted to form?

"Katie," Ruben said, touching my shoulder. "Are you all right?" There was concern in his eyes.

"Yes, yes, fine." I looked at Corine. "Well, if you're sure."

"Of course I'm sure." She waved her hand at the door again. "This isn't prison, you know, and one day when a gorgeous guy turns up to whisk *me* off into the sunset, you can stay behind and hold the fort."

"Deal." I blinked. The threat of tears thankfully had come to nothing. "I'll just grab my bag from the office then."

C h a p t e r E i g h t

It was like nothing I'd ever experienced before. A sound that didn't just make itself heard through my ears but through every cell of my body, from the soles of my feet to the tiny hairs on my arms. Every part of me got blasted by it.

As for seeing the Formula One car as it sped under us—we were standing on a black-and-white bridge over Silverstone racetrack—it was nothing more than a blur with wheels and a streak of blood red. How anyone could drive that fast and stay in control was beyond me.

"What do you think?" Ruben shouted, spinning to watch the car speed away.

I did the same, and he slipped his arm about my waist and steadied me. A gust of wind dragging behind the car had whipped my hair over my face and caused me to falter. Every bit of me was still vibrating, and the roar echoed through my head and in my chest.

"Really bloody loud," I shouted. "Is there just the one?" I glanced over my shoulder, wondering if there was more I needed to brace myself for.

"Looks like it. The McLaren team has arrived a day before everyone else. Clever move. It means they get a couple of hours on the track tonight. Could put them a step ahead."

"Why are they here?"

"It's the Grand Prix next weekend. They've just come in from Japan."

"And that's what you used to do?" I could just make out the car in the distance now, weaving around a set of snake-like bends. "Travel with the team?"

"Yes. I was one of four lead mechanics working for Dean Cudditch. That'll be him driving now."

"Dean Cudditch… I've heard of him."

"I should think you have. He's won more Grand Prix titles than any other driver."

"Wow, and you were part of that?"

Ruben gestured down at the track. "Yes, that was my home when we were racing in England — that pit stop there."

A layby gave way to a white building with a flat roof. Blue paint on the floor outlined a car-sized square surrounded by black electrical ropes and a white box, like a fuel dispenser. Several men wandered about in red all-in-one outfits. A nervous-looking man in a suit glanced at the track then studied his watch then stared at the track again.

"Come on," Ruben said. "I'll introduce you to the team."

"Really?"

"Yeah, really. They're good fun. I haven't caught up with them in months, so it will be cool to say hi."

"Er, okay."

A sudden wave of anxiety crashed through me. Ruben wanted to introduce me to the men he used to live the high life with. The guys who saw him having fun with lots of women — glamorous, gorgeous, sophisticated women from all over the world.

I frowned down at my black trousers and plain black shirt, wishing, for the first time, my work outfit wasn't so widow-like.

Ruben kept his arm around my waist as we went down the steps to the inner sanctum of the racetrack. It seemed he still had access-all-areas status, even though he wasn't working here. The two security men we'd seen had both shaken his hand, told him he looked well and smiled broadly at us.

"Hey, it's Strong," a man called out as we approached the pit stop along a marked pedestrian walkway.

"Jones, how are you doing, mate?" Ruben shouted.

Jones gripped Ruben's hand and clasped his shoulder at the same time. "You look great. Life's obviously treating you well." He grinned at me and appeared about to say something, but the deafening rumble of the car pealed through the air.

We all turned to see it popping down the gears then roll to a halt within the blue-painted square on the ground.

"We're just finishing up," Jones said. "Dean was desperate to try out a set of new high-traction tires since the track is so dry."

"Sounds like a good idea," Ruben said.

Four mechanics were around the hatch of the car, then suddenly, as the engine went silent, the driver jumped out. Tall and lean, wearing a red leather suit with McLaren written in white on the arms and legs, he tugged off his helmet.

I recognized him. Even if Ruben hadn't mentioned Dean Cudditch, I would have known it was him. His jet-black hair, trademark crew cut and small, dark goatee was known the world over.

He spotted Ruben instantly. His face lit up and he strode over, passing his helmet to someone as he went.

"Bloody hell, Ruben. I didn't know you were dropping in."

"Just passing," Ruben said.

He dropped his arm from my waist. I missed his touch.

I thought the two men would shake but they embraced, slapping each other on the back and smiling broadly.

"You look much better than last time I saw you," Dean said. "How's the new ticker?"

"Perfect." Ruben smiled and weaved his fingers with mine. "I wanted to bring Katie here. Show her what I used to do."

Dean inclined his head, studied me and nodded. "Ah, I can see why you have a sparkle back in your eye, mate. A beautiful woman on your arm is the best medicine."

I smoothed my free hand down my black clothes. Shifted from one foot to the other.

Ruben squeezed my fingers. "I agree with that."

"Nice to meet you, Katie." Dean extended his hand. He was smiling, his tanned skin was flushed and there was a horizontal groove on his forehead his helmet had left.

"You too," I said. "Though I think you bruised my eardrums."

He smiled. "Whoops, sorry. I suppose we kind of get used to it." He pointed at the car. "It's going well, even though we got soaked in Japan last week. It did nothing but rain."

"Not good, all that water." Ruben shook his head. "I watched the race. You aced Farrah."

"Yeah, only just." Dean put his hand on his hip. "Could have done with you there. You always got the tension perfect in wet weather."

"Ah, these guys are great." Ruben grinned and pointed at the men fussing over the car.

Dean followed his gaze. "Yeah, they are. But I live in hope you'll join us again."

Ruben laughed. "Maybe one day."

"I suppose that'll have to appease me for now." Dean gripped Ruben's shoulder again. "Listen, I have to go, but we're staying at the usual place. Why don't you come for dinner one night this week? Catch up with everyone? The team would love to see you."

"Yeah, I will. Wednesday probably."

"Perfect." Dean smiled at me. "Great to meet you, Katie, and whatever you're doing with my good friend here, keep doing it. It's clearly working."

* * * *

"Do you want to come up?" I asked Ruben when he parked in front of my flat an hour later. "I could make us something to eat."

He switched off the engine. "If you're sure."

I shrugged. "I'm actually quite hungry, so I'm definitely going to eat tonight."

He studied me. "Don't you eat every night?"

I looked away, concentrated on a child zipping along the pavement atop a bright pink scooter with shiny tassels on the handlebars. "No."

"You should."

"Well, I know that." I turned to him with a frown. "It's just sometimes I get tired of forcing myself to eat."

"Maybe you should stick to cream cakes. That seemed to go down well enough." He lifted his eyebrows.

My mouth watered at the memory. "Mmm, and picnics... Those dips and sandwiches you did yesterday were delicious."

Ruben tugged his keys from the ignition. "There were lots of delicious flavors on that picnic. You being one of them."

I tapped him playfully on the arm. "You're silly."

"And you're tasty." He laughed, a full belly laugh that rumbled around the car. "And yes, I will come up, just to make sure you eat. I feel it's my duty."

* * * *

I bustled about in the kitchen making pasta with tuna and a side salad. Ruben poured us each a glass of water and set the table. He then sat on the sofa, remote control in his hand, and flicked through the channels.

My new flat felt alive, as if it was a real home. The sweet, grassy breeze ambled from the living room to the kitchen. The pan on the stove was bubbling away, creating steam that clung to the window. The tangy smell of the onions I'd fried filled my nose. I could hear the TV—only the news, someone talking—but knowing Ruben was in the living room, that it wouldn't be empty and soulless when I moved from one room to the other, created a feeling of hope in me—one that made me warm and content for the first time in a long time.

I also felt I knew Ruben better for having seen a glimpse into his old life. Understood how much he'd had to change because of his illness. Maybe he was right. Perhaps he would go back to his old job one day — return to a wild, hedonistic, fast life of racing and globetrotting and leggy women with perfect bodies. I couldn't show him my old life, or ever go back to it, but it had been nice to see his.

I flicked the pasta off the boil and stood in the kitchen doorway, one hand on the frame, pushing my hair from my face with the other.

Ruben looked up. Stared at me. He pulled in a deep breath and frowned.

"Are you okay?" I asked.

"Yes, I…"

I didn't move. "What?"

"It's just…"

"Tell me?"

He smiled. "You'll think I'm being stupid."

"No I won't."

"I had a dream last night. It just came back to me, really vivid."

"What was it about?" I straightened.

"You."

"Me?" I couldn't deny the little thrill that word gave me, to think I'd been in this handsome man's dream.

"You were stood, just like that, in a doorway, holding the side, fiddling with your hair."

"Whose doorway?"

He silenced the TV. Put the remote on the tall table by the sofa. "Mine. My bedroom."

"I see."

He trailed his gaze down my body. Licked his lips.

"And what was I wearing?" I asked. Part of me was desperate to know, the other part afraid to ask. This was a new way for me to be with anyone other than Matt.

"White," he said. "You were in white."

"A dress?"

He smiled, shook his head. "Oh, no, white stockings with lace around your thighs. White teeny, tiny knickers and a corset-style top, you know, that…" He put his cupped hands on his chest and smiled. "That made you look really pretty here."

"Sounds like a very detailed dream."

"It was. It was hot." He nodded, bit on his bottom lip. "*You* were hot."

A tremble started in my stomach and moved lower. Ruben thought I was hot. Hot enough to dream in detail about me. That in itself was like being kissed passionately. It turned my attraction for him to top level. It made me feel like the woman I had been once.

I even remembered a white outfit like that. It was something I'd taken on honeymoon to surprise Matt with one night. I could almost see his face again. His eyes instantly heavy with lust, his lips moist where he'd licked them the moment I'd appeared in the doorway.

Ruben was wearing the same look now, and he shifted on the sofa the same way Matt had shifted on the bed.

Taking a deep breath, I walked toward Ruben, wishing I had on that outfit, and straddled his lap. I dug my knees into the cushions and I rested my hands on his shoulders, let my bum settle on his thighs.

"Tell me more?" I said in what I hoped was a suitably sexy voice.

Ruben swallowed, frowned a little and looked into my eyes. "We were alone. There was only us. It was warm. You smelled of fruit — papaya, melon, all things sweet."

I smiled. "This is a very specific dream."

He touched my cheek with the back of his index finger. "I know, and it's all flooding back to me like it's a real memory."

"Maybe we should make it real, one day."

"I'd like that." He leaned forward and touched his lips to mine. "You have no idea how gorgeous you are, do you?" he asked with a smile.

"I'm not gorgeous. Not really."

He jerked his head. "Why would you say that?"

"Well, the women you must have had, you know, when you and Dean Cudditch were out together, swanning around glamorous places…"

"That was just fun. Messing about, there was never anyone serious. I was too busy traveling the world, being part of the winning team."

"But weren't they…?"

"They weren't you, Katie. Matt must have told you all the time how beautiful you are. I get the impression from you that he was a great bloke, a wonderful husband who made you feel special and treasured."

I nodded. "He was. He did, but…" I glanced downward, kept that delicate balance of mine on the straight and narrow. "But now… Well, I'm a bit thinner than I was and smiles don't come so easy."

"I've seen you smile plenty since I met you, and each one has gone into my happy memory bank."

His words made me smile again.

"See? Beautiful," he said.

"Thank you. It's nice to hear someone say that."

"It's nice to have a sexy woman sitting on my lap." He kissed me, softly, and stroked his fingers through my hair.

I broke the kiss and touched his hair too. I loved the longish strands and the way they flowed through my fingers like fluid silk.

He slid his hands down the column of my neck and reached for the first button on my work blouse. As he undid it, his smile slipped, and his eyebrows hung heavy in concentration. My heart tripped. My nipples tightened. The dark look in his eyes was so sexy it went straight to my head, like a shot of alcohol.

He undid the next button and the next, his jaw seeming to get tenser with each twist of his fingers. I sat absolutely still, the tops of his thighs pressing into the backs of mine, watching his face, each blink, each slight twitch of his cheek and the way he dampened his lower lip with the tip of his tongue. It was all making me want to grab him for a kiss but equally kept me frozen, fascinated.

When all the buttons were undone, he looked up at my face. It was a silent question.

I glanced out of the window—nothing but treetops.

I nodded.

Carefully, he slid the blouse off my shoulders, revealing my white lacy bra. It had a small daisy in the center of the cups and one at the base of each strap.

"That's so much better than my dream," he whispered, his breath like a caress on my chest. "And you are perfect."

Words danced on my tongue. Words that wanted to explain that I used to be a cup size bigger and filled out my bra better. That maybe I would again one day. But I held them in, swallowed them down. They had no place in this moment with Ruben. Besides, he looked happy with what he saw.

I reached behind myself, unclipped the hook of my bra, let it fall open, but then held it in place with one arm across my chest.

"Katie, if you want to wait…?"

"No, this is fine. More than fine, I want this." I let the straps slide off my arms and tossed the bra to the floor. "It feels right with you."

And it did. I'd worried that I'd feel like an adulterous woman being with another man. But with Ruben… Well, it was different. Matt was part of it. Part of Ruben. Part of us.

Ruben collected the slight weight of the undersides of my breasts in his hands. Watching his own movements, he parted his lips and his features softened. His touch was electric and sent a plethora of forgotten sensations blasting through my chest, spiking my nipples and making my flesh feel heavy and engorged. I pressed into him, just a little, needing more but not wanting to appear greedy. Fearing if I did that, I'd push myself into a wall and cause the bubble to shatter.

He rubbed his thumbs over my nipples. They were tiny points, erect and tight. I stuttered in a breath, the stimulation arousing and wonderful.

He glanced up at me. "Are you okay?"

I nodded. "Yes, I like you touching me."

"I like touching you." The left side of his mouth rose into a languid half grin.

He moved his right hand to the center of my back. Held me firm as he leaned forward and took my left nipple into his mouth.

I gasped and ran my hands into his hair, pulled him close and arched my spine. Damn, it had been so long since I'd enjoyed this feeling. It was heavenly.

Releasing a breath, I watched as the huff of air from my lungs shifted the hair on the top of his head. He switched to the other breast, feeding my nipple into his mouth and tweaking it with his tongue. He massaged and squeezed the now damp breast he'd just given attention.

A type of fever was growing in me, but it was fever of the good kind. Between my legs felt heavy, needy. I had the urge to shift just a fraction farther forward in Ruben's lap and see if the erection I suspected was there was as hard as it had been yesterday.

I stayed still.

Ruben kissed up my sternum, my neck, and found my mouth. He was still fondling my right breast as he kissed me, wetly, hungrily and with a little less control than yesterday.

Running my hand down his chest and over his belly, I then found his groin. The folds of denim could do nothing to hide the swell of his hard cock. I itched to hold it, release it—learn the shape and weight of him the way he'd just done to me. I popped the top button, but as I did so, he grabbed my wrist, pulled back from our kiss.

"Katie," he said a little breathless.

"What's wrong?" I stilled.

He looked away.

"We can be ourselves together," I whispered. "Tell me."

"I like that." He carefully pinched my chin with his fingers and thumb.

"What?"

"That there is a 'we'. Us together."

"Me too." I grazed my lips over his. "So tell me."

He nodded and released my wrist. "It's just... Well, I want you to do whatever it is you want to do, but..."

He shut his eyes, as though frustrated with himself.

"But what?"

"But, well…I won't deny it. I'm a bit anxious, you know, about doing this—with this." He placed his hand on his chest.

"With your new heart?"

He nodded.

I took hold of the bottom of his T-shirt and peeled it up and over his head, threw it down by my bra. "This heart," I said, placing a kiss over his scar, "is a good, strong heart that can handle me just fine."

"I'm sure it will be okay. It's just…"

"You want to take it slow?" I shrugged. "I want to take it slow too. We don't have to go all the way—not if it's too soon. We can have some other fun."

"God, you must think I'm a wimp." A flash of wounded pride crossed his face.

"There's nothing wimpy about that package you've got in your pants, mister. It's feeling like a whole lot of hot, hard man to me."

He laughed. "You always say the right thing. You know that?"

I smiled and pressed my palm over his cock, squeezed through the denim.

His face fell serious. "That feels good. Your hand on me."

"I can make it feel even better, if you want me to."

He paused then nodded. "Yes. That's what I want."

I wriggled and slipped between his legs, so mine were folded on the floor and my shoulders were between his thighs. I began to undo the buttons on his jeans. I felt tiny nestled between his long limbs.

"You have…" A sudden panic gripped me.

"What?" He clenched his fists that were resting on his thighs.

I had to say it. But how could I soften it? Make it fluffy and socially acceptable? I couldn't. "You have made yourself come since the operation, though?" I'd done a first-aid course last year with my work. But still...

He touched my hair. "Yes, don't worry. It works fine. It's just you, having you here, doing whatever you're going to do..." He frowned, rubbed his chin. "Even before my op, you'd have had my blood pressure going through the roof, Katie. You're so damn sexy."

I released the last button on his fly. I wasn't that sexy, and if he'd masturbated and all was well, then what was the problem? "In that case, it will be fine. Just enjoy." I was impatient to see him, touch him. My mouth was watering. I wanted to taste him—learn his scent, shape and texture.

He lifted his hips and helped me tug down his jeans. His white CK boxers came too and his erection sprang free.

My breaths were fast and shallow. His dark cock was long and traced with bulging veins. I couldn't help but compare him to Matt, who had been shorter but thicker. Also, Ruben was circumcised, the shiny, smooth head a perfect flare and the groove beneath deep.

Very gently I took him in my fist and rubbed my thumb through that dip of silky skin beneath his glans. I was rewarded with Ruben's soft moan.

"Is that okay?" I asked, glancing up at him.

His cheeks were flushed. He nodded.

I tipped forward, swept my tongue over the tip, dipping into his slit then laving around the head.

"Oh, fuck..." he said, slotting both of his hands into my hair, his fingers just pulling on the roots, tugging my scalp in a way that far from slowed me but turned me on all the more.

I stretched my mouth wide and took the entire head of him in deep, still playing and exploring with my tongue.

"Katie," he gasped.

I withdrew, traced a particularly thick vein with my thumb. "Do you want me to stop?"

"Hell no."

I smiled, tickled my fingers through the pubic hair at the base of his belly and took him into my mouth. Feeling the smooth tip of his cock running over my palate and hitting the flat of my tongue at the back of my throat was glorious.

He groaned in a deliciously decadent way. It was the noise of a man who'd been denied a woman's mouth for years. I was pleased it was me here with him. More than pleased, I felt privileged. I withdrew, sank back down and set up a steady rhythm with my hand and mouth. My pussy was hot—my clit pressing against my knickers—each slight movement rubbing it and making it greedy for stimulation. Ruben's body was stiff, his legs holding me secure and his abs a sheet of steel. I ran my free hand up to his chest, felt for his heartbeat. It was thudding away, fast and strong.

"Oh, oh, I'm going to... Katie." His shifted his hips, toward my mouth, then bucked away, as though overwhelmed.

But I didn't let him escape. If anything, I increased my enthusiasm—sucked and swirled, intensified my grip on the root of his shaft, holding it tight in the circle of my index finger and thumb and dragging up and down to meet my lips.

"I'm gonna come in your mouth if you're not careful," he said, fisting my hair.

That was the idea, but I didn't pause to tell him that. Instead, I found his balls with my fingertips, so I was cupping the base of his shaft and rolling him too. Saliva dripped down my chin, lubricating the way, heating us further.

"Ah, ah, ah, yes, yes," he hissed.

His cock was bone-hard and swollen as I felt the first pulse of release.

Cum flooded the back of my throat. I swallowed, kept working him with my mouth and touching his balls. Another shot swamped my tongue. I guzzled it, loving his flavor, the salty thickness of his pleasure.

He clasped a hand over mine, the one that was flat on his chest. "Jesus, that's so fucking good," he gasped. "Fucking hell, ah, oh yeah…"

I slowed and relaxed my grip. He unclamped his legs from around me.

I caught his cock in my hand and looked up.

He was staring down at me, red-cheeked and with a sheen of sweat on his brow and upper lip. His heart was pounding. His breaths were coming out rapid. His hair had flopped forward.

"That worked okay for you?" I asked, releasing him and wiping moisture from my chin.

"More than okay. Bloody hell, Katie…that was…"

Suddenly I was on his lap again. He'd hoisted me up beneath my arms and sat me sideways. His sudden speed and strength both surprised and thrilled me.

I looped my hands behind his neck and felt his softening cock against my hip.

"Thank you," he said, touching my lips with the tips of his fingers, following their shape, from one corner to the other and dipping into my cupid's bow.

I smiled. "I had fun." I stroked down his neck to his chest, touched his scar. Matt's heart was still thudding, thudding because of the orgasm I'd just given Ruben.

"Damn, I'm tingling all over," Ruben said, touching the layer of dampness on his brow.

"Is that a bad sign?" Shit, what had I done? Had I finished him off with a blow job?

He laughed. "No, good tingling. Long-overdue tingling."

"Phew." I smiled and kissed him through my grin.

"I feel I should return the favor." He ran his hand over my shoulder, found my breast and fondled my nipple.

The offer was very appealing. I, too, was tingling with desire, a lust for more skin-on-skin and feeling Ruben hit that high again, with me in tow. But I also believed that what we had was delicate and new and we'd said we'd go slow. "Maybe another time," I said.

"I feel like I could run a marathon. Don't worry about me. I'm fine — more than fine."

I pulled away. "But what about slow? Us taking it slow?"

"I've always loved speed. Fast cars..." He winked. "Fast women..."

"I've noticed." I giggled but kept my head drawn back. "But still, we should eat."

He stilled his movements, then released my nipple and stroked his hand up to my cheek. "Okay, I hear you. But I should warn you I'm not the type of bloke who likes to be in debt. It just doesn't sit well with me."

I untangled myself and stood. "That's great to know because I'm not a woman who likes to be owed."

"Perfect match then." He shuffled on the sofa, tugged up his boxers and jeans. He reached for my bra and blouse, handed them to me. "Much as I'd like to eat dinner with you like that." He nodded at my bare chest. "You might get your due quicker than you want."

Chapter Nine

My new home was silent as I stared in the mirror and applied scarlet lipstick that matched the flowers on my top. Dragging the color around, I thought of my lips on Ruben. Matt's heart had pumped blood through his body at a furious rate as I'd made him come. Matt's lungs had heaved air in and out of Ruben's chest, making him pant and gasp and stretch out a delicious moan that I could still hear whenever I summoned the memory.

I hadn't seen Ruben for several days. After we'd hungrily demolished the pasta dish we'd cuddled and kissed in the hallway then he'd left.

I'd lain awake half the night, wondering if I should have let him 'return the favor', as he'd put it. It would have led to more. I was sure of it. How could it not? Ultimately it would have also led to him staying the night.

Was I ready for that? A new man in my bed?

A few weeks ago my answer would have been a definite no. But with Ruben... Well, it was different. He was connected to Matt. He made me feel closer to

Matt. Ruben was Ruben, a man who'd become important to me in a short space of time, yet someone who I felt had been waiting for me as much as I'd been searching for him.

I put away the lipstick and felt a now familiar bubble of pleasure pop inside me. That had been one hell of a sexy moment. I'd replayed it over more times than I could count.

And it hadn't been Matt I'd been thinking of as I'd sucked Ruben off. Not at all. I was there, with Ruben, this new man, with a new body for me to discover — what he liked, how he felt, his taste, what he could do with *his* mouth. I was definitely with Ruben. I didn't feel as if I was being unfaithful to Matt. It was as if he were there, approving of us.

Would he, though?

I shut the living room window then grabbed my keys off the side of the hall dresser. Let myself out of the flat. I was meeting Janine in half an hour and a group of her friends she'd assured me I'd just adore. They were 'a scream' apparently.

Matt would have wanted me to be happy, that I knew in a very real, central part of my soul. We'd been a strong, united couple, completely unselfish in every decision we'd made. If it had been the other way round and I'd died, I would have wanted him to find someone to share the rest of his life with. Living without love was a map of gray nothingness. Being lonely like flailing through space without a destination.

But would I have wanted him to end up with a woman who had my actual, physical heart?

I tightened the strap of my small red bag over my shoulder, quickened my pace. How could I possibly know the answer to that question? What were the chances of it ever happening?

But my chances had been high, the odds with me because I'd manipulated it so Ruben and I *had* met.

But it hadn't been out of maliciousness, just curiosity. Macabre curiosity maybe, but that was all — a need to know. And I hadn't ever wanted to talk to him, certainly not date him, and absolutely, definitely not suck his cock. Not back then. All I'd wanted to do was see him, from a distance. Make sure he was okay and that Matt's heart was serving him well. I'd just needed to be able to picture where that bit of Matt was when I lay in bed at night, missing him more than I'd miss all four of my limbs if they were torn from me.

I turned off the avenue onto the main street into town, dodging an old man walking two Dalmatians.

No, Matt would understand, I was sure of it. He'd gotten my whacky, impetuous ways. Had laughed at the same kooky things that made me giggle. Thought out of the box when he'd needed to in order to follow my sometimes back-to-front reasoning. My own heart felt content with my deal with Matt, at peace. He'd understand why I was doing this. I was sure he would.

The bar where I was meeting Janine and her friends came into view. The Slippery Slope, it was called, and it had bright orange window frames and ornate black lamps hanging either side of the door. It was sandwiched between a dry cleaners and a hairdresser. Above looked like offices.

Could I ever tell anyone what I'd done? 'Hey, meet my boyfriend, he has my dead husband's heart and lungs. That's cool, isn't it?' A rush of nausea gripped me, and I paused, took a deep breath. It wasn't cool, and it was hardly dinner table conversation.

They'd all think I was mad. Maybe I was. Since meeting Ruben, my mind had been a swirl of emotions, a heady soup of longing, craving, satisfaction and a bright new feeling of optimism. Now I wasn't having to pretend to laugh or smile. It was just happening. Each step through the day wasn't like wading through a tide of treacle. Some of the time I was even walking normally, without being weighed down by that damn anvil.

It was something I could get used to, and I sure as hell wasn't about to give it up.

There was nothing for it. What Ruben had — and what had been my decision to give him — would have to remain a secret. Something kept hidden in that locked box, along with the guilt.

No one knew I'd found him except for the private detective, who was sworn to confidentiality. Only one person, Melanie, my old boss, had ever known of my desperate hankering to meet the recipient who had Matt's heart. That was because of a drunken night out when I'd ended up crying, her holding me and my blurting out how much it would mean to me to meet that person. But she wouldn't even remember that muddled conversation. She'd been as sloshed on wine as I had been. That was in the past. History. Another time and place. Besides, I was in Northampton now. Forty miles away. I had new friends to make, a new life to live.

I looked at The Slippery Slope again. Several people wandered in, laughter and music filtered out. It was a young person's pub, so how come I felt old?

Maybe I was. Maybe I'd aged. Pain could do that.

"You all right, love?" A deep voice came from my right.

I turned. A group of several men, all in jeans and short-sleeved shirts wandered past. One with blond hair was grinning at me as he walked, hands shoved into his jeans pockets.

"Yes," I said.

"Maybe catch you for a drink in The Slippery?" He nodded ahead and smiled wider. He had dazzling blue eyes and a small diamond earring.

I pushed my hair over my shoulders. "I'm meeting friends."

"Ah," he said. "A man can still hope."

"Come on, Romeo." His mate banged him on the shoulder. "She's well out of your league."

"I know." Blond Guy shrugged and winked at me. "Hope is always worth hanging on to though."

They wandered off. Again, I paused. The blond man was cute — a hot bum neatly encased in denim, and broad shoulders accentuated by a fitted shirt. But whilst I could appreciate a fine specimen, I suddenly wished Ruben was with me, that he was at my side to give me a quick smile and squeeze my hand before I met these new people.

I adored the way his eyes narrowed when he grinned and the way tiny lines creased at the corners. His lips were familiar now, too — their shape, their taste, how they moved when he spoke and laughed. I was missing him this week. I hoped he was having a nice night out with his old teammates, chatting about wild days gone by, but still, I was looking forward to the next time I saw him smile, heard his voice, felt his arms around me.

I summoned my courage and, shoving aside a trespassing thought about turning around and going home, I walked up to The Slippery Slope.

I'd just put my hand on the door when I heard my mobile phone beep. Quickly I stepped sideways, not entering the pub but standing beneath one of the large black lamps out of the way of other drinkers moving in and out. I plucked my phone from my bag. It was a message from Ruben. A lovely little shiver, almost a caress, tickled the base of my neck and settled in my chest. I hit *Open*.

Hope you're having a great time with new friends. Looking forward to seeing you Friday. Shall we snuggle up on the back row of the cinema and eat popcorn? The new Bond movie looks amazing. X

I read it twice. Had he been missing me at the same time I was hankering for him? I tapped a quick reply.

Just about to meet Janine and her friends. Cinema sounds great. I'll check out the times. X

After hitting *Send*, I slipped the phone away. As soon as I did, another text message came through.

They'll love you. See you Friday. X PS I'm still on a high from the other night!

I smiled and let warmth that had nothing to do with the balmy evening wrap around me. Suddenly, instead of feeling nervous, I felt positive again. I'd always been fine meeting new people in the past. Got on with everyone, no problems, but tonight, I couldn't deny that I did feel nervous. *They'll love you*, was the right thing to say and also how Matt would have reassured me.

And as for still being on a high, well, I could understand that. I certainly was.

Quickly, I messaged back a simple…

X X

Then pushed into the bar.

Noisy chatter and the tangy mix of cologne, perfume and beer hit me, as did the swarm of bodies and the thud of music.

"Katie, Katie, over here."

I spun at the sound of my name, peered past several sets of shoulders and spotted Janine waving from a curved bench by the window. Three other females sat with her, all with wine in front of them and wide smiles on their faces.

This would be fine. I knew it would be.

Hope, after all, was worth hanging on to.

* * * *

It seemed to take forever for Friday to come around. Despite having had a lovely time on Wednesday with Janine, April, Mia and Sarah, then an upbeat two-hour conversation with my parents on Thursday about my move and a plan to visit them soon, time—in my mind—had distorted and it felt as if the hours were days.

The girls, as Janine referred to them, had been a hoot, and there'd been a laugh a minute when the conversation had gotten raunchy late into the evening—wine loosening tongues and wiping out inhibitions. I'd listened, enjoying their frankness about sex and the fact that I didn't feel so out of the game. I had a tall, dark and handsome boyfriend now, so Janine had been quick to tell them, who had collected me from Skin Deep and whisked me away.

Just talking about Ruben made me smile—one of the lovely, easy smiles that I didn't have to concentrate on and that didn't hurt a bit. I'd nodded and said we were heading to the cinema to see the new Bond film for our next date. This had then started a conversation about which Bond they'd 'do', given the choice—Daniel Craig being the most popular.

But now it was Friday, and I was hovering in my hallway, waiting for Ruben.

I flicked off an electric fan I'd had running since I'd gotten in from work, blowing air through the flat. The heat was as intense as it had been for the last few weeks, but today the humidity had cranked up several notches. The atmosphere felt damp, the weight of it oppressive. Perhaps we'd have a storm to re-align the equilibrium.

The doorbell rang. I took a last glance in the mirror and touched the silver necklace I was wearing. It had a small butterfly hanging from it.

I pulled open the door.

"Hey, gorgeous," Ruben said.

A sweep of shyness tickled my insides. He was so damn good-looking. But before I could do anything about my bashfulness, I was in his arms and he was kissing me.

I parted my lips, let him touch his tongue to mine. Closed my eyes and soaked up his fruity, sexy scent as I breathed him in. His shoulders were high and hard, and I gripped them, loving the feel of his long body against mine after missing him all week.

Eventually he paused for breath. "We should go. I have tickets." He kissed my cheek then touched the damp patch with his thumb.

I straightened his collar and let go of him, stepped back with a smile. "Yes, we should." I reached for my keys. It was tempting to suggest we skip the Bond film. Stay home and let him settle his debt. I was sure he'd be up for it. But maybe later… Right now I just wanted to be with him. Enjoy the lightness that Ruben's presence injected into me. He was like a balm to my soul, a very wounded, hurt part of my soul that needed nurturing back to health.

We walked out onto the street, and Ruben linked our fingers.

I was about to make a comment about the heat and the ominous-looking black clouds peeking above the rooftops, when he held my left hand aloft and studied it.

"You've taken your wedding ring off," he said.

"Yes. It's been off a while now."

We carried on walking.

He kept our fingers weaved but dropped our hands back down.

"Are you okay with that?" he asked.

"It suddenly felt right."

"You didn't…" He hesitated. "Take it off because of me, did you? Shit. Sorry, that makes me sound like I'm full of my own self-importance." He shook his head and frowned, bit on his bottom lip. "It's just I had no problem with you wearing it, that's all."

"No. It was for me. My new start here. I didn't want to be seen as a sad person anymore. I wanted to just be Katie again. Be able to smile and have fun without people looking at me and thinking that it was good that I was getting over Matt's death."

Ruben was silent. We continued on our way.

"Because I don't think I'll ever get over losing him, you know."

He turned to me, frown still in place. "It must have been so hard."

I steadied my balance, kept putting one foot in front of the other on that thin rope my emotions walked on. "Losing my husband was the single most awful thing that has ever happened to me. Nothing could compare. Living with that is hard enough. Living with people feeling sorry for me became unbearable. It made it impossible to move on."

"I know what you mean. Sort of."

"Yes, you probably do. People, your teammates and friends, must have seen you differently once you became ill?"

"Yes, they did. I wasn't Ruben—the fastest, strongest member of the team anymore—the bloke who could party all night, sink pints quicker than anyone else then still think on my feet when the engine developed problems midrace." He sighed. "It was hard, that change in the perception people had of me. Made me feel less of a man, like my body had let me down."

"It had."

"Yep, big time. Facing my mortality was like a boulder crashing toward me. One that I couldn't get out the way of, you know, like in *Indiana Jones* when he's running out of the cave with that huge rock rolling after him." He huffed. "I was knocking on death's door. There was no doubt about it, and all in the space of a year or so. Bad luck had never been so bad as far as I was concerned." He lifted my hand again, looked at my naked finger with its fading pale stripe. "So do you feel like you're not married to him anymore?"

I thought of my ring, nestled safely in my purse.

"I should have asked that the other night, before…" Ruben squeezed my fingers a little. "Sorry."

"No apologies. I wouldn't have... Well, I wouldn't have...you know...if I still felt married. But it's more complicated than that. I don't feel unmarried."

"What do you mean?"

"Well, it's not like we stopped loving each other and went separate ways. He left, but not because he wanted to, because of that damn bad luck you were talking about."

We paused and crossed the road.

Once safely on the other side and with the cinema in view, I continued, "Till death do us part. That was what we promised each other. We've parted. I accept that now, and I've also accepted that I'll never stop loving him, but the heart is a wonderful thing..." I glanced at Ruben as a whip of wind picked up and flattened his gray polo shirt to his pectoral muscles and flat stomach. "There's lots of room for love in any one heart. Of that I'm certain."

Chapter Ten

We walked from the dark auditorium into the cinema lobby. The Bond movie had been everything it promised to be—full of action, hot men, sexy ladies and a blast of explosions at the end. Ruben had stayed true to his word, and we'd snuggled on the back row in specially designed seats for couples—without the armrests—and munched our way through an enormous tub of butter popcorn.

Stepping outside into the dark street, I felt a flurry of cool air flick my hair, wrapping it around my cheek.

"Whoa, it's getting wild," I said, ducking my head and wishing I'd brought a jacket.

"Shall we get a taxi?" Ruben asked, pointing at a queue of about nine couples waiting at the empty rank.

"No, we'll be fine. It's only a few minutes, isn't it."

Ruben glanced at the sky. A streak of lightning lit the tall buildings opposite.

"We should get going," he said as a stormy gust pushed his hair from his face, sending it backward in a soft wave.

We reached for each other's hand and scurried in the direction of home. But within minutes, the first big pellets of rain hit me, soaking through my blouse and onto my skin.

"Ah, yuck," Ruben said, increasing his pace. "We're going to get seriously wet."

I jogged to keep up with him. Several raindrops struck my face, and I said a silent goodbye to my mascara.

Another bolt of lightning brought the dim street into illumination. It was closely followed by a bellow of thunder that rattled through my chest.

I squealed then laughed at my surprised reaction. Ruben tightened his grip on me and broke into a run, weaving us around the trees on the avenue and past several wheelie bins that had been put out for the next morning's collection.

Soon it was hard to see through the torrential downpour. My hair was plastered to my head, my skinny jeans stuck to my legs and my blouse splattered to my body. The rain smelled fresh as it washed away weeks of dry dust baked onto the pavement and garden walls. It felt welcomingly cool as it sloshed against me and seeped onto my flesh, finding every gulley and dip on my body to drizzle into.

Ruben turned the corner onto my street and glanced at me with a worried frown. "Are you okay?"

"Never better," I said, grinning and tugging at my sodden blouse.

He returned my smile and pushed a lick of hair from his eyes. "Come on. We're nearly there."

We splashed through puddles, pelting spray high up our legs. Another loud giggle burst from me. I felt like a kid playing out in the rain again. Purposely I headed for an extra-large puddle and stomped through it.

Ruben laughed, steered us to the next dip in the pavement, which held a large expanse of water, and we did the same again, in synchrony. Water burst upward, hitting my thighs.

A car went past, the sound of its tires on the liquid surface of the road a noise I hadn't heard for weeks. It sent a puddle arcing our way. Just before it sprayed us, the brief image of the slash of raindrops streaking in front of its headlights burned into my mind. We grabbed each other and turned away. I nestled my head in the crook of Ruben's shoulder as we hollered our fake rage at the driver for soaking us.

A fun memory logged into my new register of Katie's happy times.

Ruben hurried us along, until eventually we raced up to the entrance of my flat. We dashed in.

I was out of breath as I hunted for my key and climbed the one set of stairs to home. It was hard to see into my bag. Water was streaking down my face and my hair was hanging in rats' tails around my eyes. Eventually I found the key and shoved it into the lock.

"Phew, thank goodness," I said, stepping into my flat.

Ruben hurried in behind me and shut the door.

"I'll grab us some towels," I said, racing to the laundry pile. I retrieved a couple of freshly washed pink towels that smelled of fabric conditioner and passed one to Ruben.

He took it and dropped it over his head, rubbed vigorously. I did the same to mine and toed off my sandals at the same time. I dabbed my face, collected an oasis sitting in the groove of my throat and patted beneath my eyes, hoping I wasn't displaying a panda look.

Ruben buried his face in the towel then dropped it to one side. "I don't think I've ever got so wet so fast," he said, trying and failing to flatten his now fluffed up hair.

"It was fun," I said. "I'd forgotten how much I like to splash through puddles or how much I enjoy a good storm."

As I'd said the last word a tremendous boom, accompanied by white light, filled my flat. I jumped and let out a slightly hysterical squeak. "Well, that's maybe a bit too close for comfort."

Ruben smiled, but then the smile fell. His gaze dipped and he stepped up to me. "Did you know your blouse is see-through?"

"Is it?" I glanced down, automatically pressing my arm over my breasts.

He caught my hand, tugged it to my side. "The best type of blouse, as far as I'm concerned."

My white blouse had indeed turned transparent, highlighting my white cotton bra and the small pebbles my nipples had become in the cool rain. I could just make them out, dark disks beneath white material.

"Ruben, I…"

Suddenly I was face-to-face with him. He'd picked me up, arms tight around my body and our chests pressing together. My bare feet were dangling.

I put my hands on his shoulders and stared at his face. His eyelashes were still heavy with water and had become tiny triangular points. A large drip was rolling from his right temple into the fuzz of hair by his ear.

"I think it's time," he said, his lips almost touching mine, "to pay my debt."

Beneath his wet clothes, his body felt hot and hard. There was also a seriously sexy glint in his eye that held determination and lust—a delicious combination.

I pushed my hands through his damp hair and kissed him. Was vaguely aware of him walking, heading to my bedroom, as our tongues weaved together. I slanted my head, deepened the kiss, and he moaned gently, feeding me more of what I wanted.

Ruben Strong.

He set me on the edge of the bed, his mouth not leaving mine. I was wet, turned on, scared and excited. It was like living in a cloud—someone else's life—but it was mine. My life. And I was here with Ruben, gorgeous Ruben who was acting more than ready to give me what I was owed.

He kissed across my cheek, at the same time his caress roamed down my chest and my stomach, seeking out my fly button.

I tugged at his top, wanting the wet material out of our way.

He paused to fist it between his shoulder blades and drag it over his head.

His chest was beautiful, the hair damp and flat with rain, his nipples, like mine, taut and hard. I looked at the scar, smooth and pink, and the neat trail of hair that feathered across his stomach then disappeared into his jeans.

"Say yes," he said, kissing my right breast through my top and bra. "Katie, say yes."

"Yes," I murmured, lying fully back and trying to push at my trousers. "Yes, Ruben, yes."

He kneeled between my legs, helped me drag my jeans past my hips and over my buttocks, peeling away the tight material that was clinging to my skin. He worked fast, his hands gripping and tugging the denim downward.

Eventually they bunched at my ankles and with a final jerk, were off.

He shoved them aside and kissed my knee then my thigh, his lips and hands warm on my cool, damp flesh.

I dropped back on the bed again, folded my arms over my face. This was the first time I'd been this intimate with another man. Matt had always said he loved giving me oral, but would Ruben? What if I wasn't what he expected? What if all those supermodels and glamorous girls had been his type and I just wasn't up to his standard?

"Lift," he murmured, his breath a hot breeze on my lower stomach. He gripped the waistband of my little white knickers.

I did as he'd asked. Let him pull them down my legs then over first one foot then the other, my arms still over my face.

"Katie, look at me," he said, running his hands up my inner thighs, his thumbs sweeping very near my intimate folds.

I gasped, tensed.

"Katie." He stilled.

I pulled my arms away. Looked down.

He was staring up at me from between my legs, his eyes wide, pupils dilated and a hint of redness on his cheeks. "I've been thinking of this moment for days," he said. "Giving you the same pleasure you gave me, but if you don't…"

"Yes," I said, touching his cheek, the one with the mole. "I want you to. It's just…different."

"I know." He dropped a kiss to my inner thigh then shifted upward and set one over my small strip of pubic hair. "But you know you talked about 'we', us?"

"Yes."

"Then let's be us." His eyes were earnest, his longing almost tangible. "Let me make you come, Katie. Because we're so good together, and I just have to be with you, touching you, tasting you." He shut his eyes, poked out his tongue, and wound the tip into my folds, spreading the soft flesh and gently searching.

"Ahhh…" My spine stiffened. A weight grew in my pussy—a good weight, one that needed feeding.

He found my clit and created a delicious suction. He sucked some more and rotated the small bead with his tongue.

I gripped the sheet. "Oh…"

Ruben searched out my entrance, one finger toying with me in delicate strokes and probes. He pushed in, his slide to knuckle-deep easy.

Keeping my eyes open, I watched his head moving, his hair shifting and his long, straight nose burying in my mound. I curled my toes and moved my hips in time with his ministrations, loving the almost forgotten sensation of building to climax. After a few minutes he increased the pressure and the speed.

Red-hot darts of lust rocketed through me, every nerve on high alert. I let my head fall to the bed, shut my eyes and grabbed his hair. I wanted to push my pussy into his face, ride his hand. "Oh, God, yes, Ruben. Don't stop. It's so good."

He added another finger, applied pressure to my G-spot. The density of the sensations multiplied. I thrashed my head from side to side, drew up my knees and fastened them against his shoulders.

He sucked my clit harder, working it with his tongue and increasing the pace at which he pounded my G-spot with the tips of his strong fingers. The point of no return besieged me. I held my breath, allowed blackness and bliss to consume my body for a few sweeter-than-sweet seconds until an avalanche of release crashed through me.

I pulled at Ruben's hair, bowed from the bed, dug my heels into his back. I wanted more, yet it was too much. "Ah, that's it, oh, oh…"

My pussy was spasming around his buried fingers, my clit pulsing in his mouth. Soft, wet noises filled my ears, along with the sounds of my ragged breathing and racing pulse.

"Please," I said, squirming. "Please, that's it…" I needed to catch my breath, orientate myself. Damn, that had felt good. Mind-blowingly good.

He released me, pulled his fingers from my pussy and sat back on his heels.

I shunted myself onto the bed fully, pressed my legs together and flopped backward on the pillow. After allowing another orgasmic shiver to control my body, I released a whimpering sigh.

A warm glow of satisfaction nestled in my core.

Ruben was up and over me, his hand against my cheek. "Are you all right?"

"Yes, oh yes." I smiled up at him. His face was damp, his cheeks a deeper shade of red. "Thank you."

"Bloody hell, don't thank me. That was incredible. *You* are incredible. So responsive."

"Well, it's been a while. I suppose some tension had built up."

He kissed me through a self-satisfied smile, and I tasted the sweet muskiness of myself.

His wet jeans skimmed my thigh, and I touched the waistband of them and broke the kiss. "You should get out of these wet things."

"So should you." He plucked at a button on my blouse. "You'll make the bed damp."

Another shock of thunder blasted down. The window rattled as a fresh torrent of rain barraged the pane.

"It's horrible out there. Bed is the safest place for us," I said, quickly removing my top and bra. I needed skin-on-skin, the touch of his body against mine. Him leaving now wasn't an option. I'd known all along it wouldn't be.

"Good plan." He shucked off his jeans and boxers then stooped for his wallet.

"Don't worry about it," I said, guessing he was retrieving a condom.

"But...?"

"I'm on the pill. It suits me for other reasons."

He put his wallet on top of his trousers. "And we're so out of the game that we're both clean, yeah?"

I nodded, and we slipped beneath the covers as another roar tumbled across the sky and shook the lampshade.

The bottom sheet was cool on my bare skin, and the duvet fluffed over me with a waft of soap-powder-laced air. Ruben pressed up to my side, his nakedness sending a shiver of longing through my entire body.

He stopped moving against me. "Katie?"

"I'm fine." I slid my hand around his waist, turned and faced him. "I just never thought when I was with Matt that I'd one day be in bed with another man."

"I'm so sorry. I—"

"No, don't be sorry, Ruben. It's not your fault."

"I know, but if he hadn't died, I wouldn't be here."

A stutter of air caught in my throat. How true that was, but not in the way Ruben had meant it. I slid my hand from his waist up to his chest, rested the heel of my palm over his left nipple.

"Do you still feel like he's with you sometimes?" Ruben whispered, touching my cheek.

"Yes." I could feel his heart right now. "Sometimes, when I'm in that hazy moment between sleep and awake, before I remember that he's gone, I imagine he's with me and it feels so real." I gave a sad smile. "It's just my brain playing tricks on me—cruel tricks."

Ruben scrunched his eyebrows together, as though what I'd said had hurt him too. "That must be difficult."

"Yes, but..." A realization dawned on me. "It's happening less and less, since I met you." I swept my fingertips over his collarbone, drew a circle on his rounded shoulder then traced a line up his neck to the corner of his jaw. "You make me feel like I have a reason to get up in the morning again."

His eyes flicked a little as he switched his attention between mine. "And you make me feel like I truly am alive again. For so long I was just living in a wrecked shell. Even after the op, it was months before any kind of normality returned, but now...this...here." He pushed my hair back from my forehead, touched his lips to the tip of my nose. "There were plenty of times when I never thought I'd make love to a woman again—and a beautiful one at that. Right now I feel like the luckiest man on earth and I wouldn't change a thing about my past because it's all led to this moment, here with you."

A familiar tingle stung my eyes. I blinked and swallowed.

"Don't cry." He kissed my cheek, his prickly chin a tiny bit sharp.

"I— It's just complicated." I gripped his other arm, felt his biceps tense. "I'm happy to be here with you, but still, I would change Matt dying in a heartbeat."

"Of course you would. I know you would, so would I."

"But—" Would he, though? If he knew the truth?

"Shh," he said. "Let's live for the here and now and enjoy this new way to be ourselves, but together. Katie and Ruben back from hell."

"Yes." That made sense, this was the new me. Ruben was the new man in my life. There was still a connection to the old Katie, but it was Ruben holding me, touching me, comforting me. And I was bloody glad to see the back of hell—not a place I intended visiting again.

But damn, Ruben was hot. Not only that, his hard cock pressing into my thigh was beyond tempting. Despite my recent orgasm, another wave of longing rushed through me. Longing for closeness, connection—us finding our pleasure together.

"Ruben," I said, winding my legs with his and feeling the hairs on his shins tickling my flesh. "Make love to me."

He pressed his lips against mine. "With pleasure."

He shifted, and I parted my thighs, let him settle between them.

His weight above me was a fresh sensation, one I'd missed for so long I'd forgotten how it felt. He propped onto his elbows, cupped the nape of my neck in a gentle squeeze and stared down at me.

For a long moment we just looked at each other. I studied the contours of his face—the way his bottom lip was a little fuller than the top and how the stubble on his jaw swept down from that patch of hair in front of his ears and arched perfectly over his lips. He was truly gorgeous. I was a very lucky girl.

I became impatient, a sudden need for more grabbing me. I shifted my body beneath his, rubbing my breasts against his chest and resting my hands on his shoulders. "Ruben," I whispered.

He opened his mouth but said nothing. His cock nudged my entrance, and he eased in an inch.

It took some effort to force myself to relax. It had been so long, and the head of his cock was wide and hard. I felt small and tight but I wanted him so much. I tilted my hips, took him in a little bit more, even though there was a stitch of discomfort.

"Oh, you're so hot and wet and gripping me," he said, tightening his hold on the back of my head, as though keeping me just where he wanted me.

Discomfort turned to pleasure—greedy, needy pleasure. "It feels so nice," I said, tucking my ankles around the back of his thighs. "Give me more."

"Ah, baby…" He slid through my wetness and, as he did so, he shut his eyes and lifted his head, turned it to the side.

He was big and solid, and I let out a moan as the wonderful sensation of being filled consumed me. Damn, I'd missed this.

When he hit maximum depth, balls pressed up against me, we both stilled. After a few seconds he parted his lips and exhaled. His head bobbed as though he'd lost the concentration to hold it up.

I cupped his cheek, supported him and stroked the short, spiked hairs on his neck with my thumb. Bliss captured his features in slack-mouthed beauty, and I could have come just from seeing him like that. It was magical, a gift. My heart swelled with love, and I knew right then what we were doing was making love.

He pulled out a little then slowly eased back in, the same serene expression on his face.

The movement was small, but his pubis captured my clit in a luscious scrape, and I gasped, tensed my internal muscles and allowed that first spark of orgasm to flicker to life. "That's right, just there," I gasped.

"Katie," he breathed. "Damn, it's never felt...so good." He set up a steady rocking rhythm that applied the perfect pressure and massaged my G-spot too.

"Oh...oh..." I said, still cupping his cheek and now clutching his shoulder.

My body was tense, like a coiled spring. Ruben was building me up in a slow, intense grind that was driving me mad with want.

I shut my eyes and moved my head to the side, only to find my mouth captured by his in a dreamy but profound kiss. Our breaths were ragged, our lips barely under control, our bodies about to detonate.

As my orgasm claimed me, I groaned into the kiss, balanced on the precipice of ecstasy then succumbed to the demands of my climax. Pulsing through the release, my pussy a fist around Ruben's cock as he found his pleasure.

He shoved to the hilt, the only movement that had been urgent in our entire connection, and sucked in a breath that he held deep. He pumped inside me, his eyes screwed up tight and his head again twisted to the side.

Sweat popped over my body. I tightened my hold on him. Needing to be as close to him as possible.

"Ah, fucking hell yeah..." he said as he blew out the breath he'd been holding. "Katie, I..." He opened his eyes, looked down at me with a slightly stunned expression.

"That was perfect," I said.

"My thought exactly."

Chapter Eleven

When I woke the next morning, the scent of wet grass and clean air filtered in through the open window. I stretched across the bed, hoping to find Ruben, but the sheet was rumpled and cool and there was no warm body to snuggle into.

A rattle of pans and the radio flicking on in the kitchen caught my attention, and I smiled, enjoying being greeted by movement and life in my flat. Slipping eagerly from my bed, I tugged on a pair of knickers then wrapped a short, pink silk dressing gown around myself. I headed into the bathroom.

I freshened up, my body feeling a little stiff and tender. My night with Ruben had exercised muscles and stretched parts of me unused to being stretched. I smiled at my reflection, dragged a brush through my hair then brushed my teeth.

"Hey, sleepyhead," Ruben said when I wandered into the kitchen. "I'm making eggs. Is that all right with you?"

"Great." I walked up behind him.

He wore low-slung jeans, his feet and top half bare. I wrapped my arms around his waist and rested my cheek between his shoulders.

He stopped what he was doing and pressed his hands over my forearms. "Last night was incredible," he said quietly.

"I know." As I spoke, my cheek wrinkled against his back, and I smiled at how I much I adored touching him, with every part of my body on any part of his.

He turned, spinning within my arms, and hugged me close. I tipped my face to his neck, breathed in his scent, and felt the roughness of his beardy growth on my nose.

"I want to spend the day with you," he said, stroking my hair then down over the slippery material of my gown, right into the small of my back. "It's the Grand Prix. I have hospitality tickets. How do you fancy it?"

I looked up at him. "I can't. I'm going to Leicester. My friend Felicity is getting married next month and it's the hen party tonight. I would cancel, but Melanie—that's my old boss—she rang yesterday to make sure I was still going and is expecting me to stay at hers."

His face dropped for a second, but then he smiled. "That sounds like fun. It will be good for you to see your old friends."

"I think so." I hoped so. I'd touched the edge of happiness again and I was reluctant for the spell to be broken by stepping back into my previous life—being the old, sad Katie. I didn't want her to come back to Northampton with me, thinking it was okay to move in like an unwelcome guest.

"It *will* be." He pinched my chin in his fingers and thumb. "Those hen parties always look pretty wild. You can let your hair down."

"I'd rather be with you."

"And I'd rather be with you, but hey, maybe tomorrow?"

I untangled myself from him, stepped away and into the dining area. Looked at the photograph of my wedding day. A balloon of sadness grew in my chest, but I didn't let it overwhelm me. I contained it. Now was not the time.

Ruben rested his hand on my shoulder, his fingers light but comforting.

"It would have been his birthday tomorrow," I said. "I think I'll go and see his parents before I drive back to Northampton. It would be the right thing to do."

"That sounds a good idea." He squeezed my shoulder.

I touched his hand with mine, kept it there. I wanted to be with Ruben, really I did, but tomorrow I knew I'd be in a dark place. Those shadows would creep from the corners of my mind, twist themselves around my grief and tug it back into the forefront.

I needed to be alone, or at least with just my memories. But only tomorrow then I'd let my new life pour light over me again. It would be okay. I had some new happy memories to help chase away the darkness.

"How about Monday?" I asked. "I'm on a half day at the shop."

"Well, I'm working, but come up to the museum. We'll go to the Park Café and get some lunch, and then I'll show you those pictures I've just reframed."

"Won't your boss mind?"

"Boss? No, there's no real boss. I suppose it's me if you look at the payroll, but it's all so relaxed that most of the staff are horizontal. The opposite to life on the track."

"Then I'd like that, to come to your work." I carried on looking at the photograph. Felt Ruben's breath shift my hair and the heat from his chest radiate onto my back.

"He looks a nice bloke," Ruben said quietly. "Someone I'd be mates with."

"Yes, he would have liked you." I had a sudden image of Ruben and Matt sitting in a pub, full pints in their hands and cheering on some football match or Formula One race. They both had easy smiles, kind eyes and a certain masculine quality that worked just right for me, pushed my buttons.

"He was big," Ruben said.

"He liked to workout at the gym and play rugby at weekends. Plus his job was very physical." I looked at Matt's shoulders, wide and broad beneath his suit jacket. I could still feel them, remember what they were like to hang on to if he swung me into his arms or if I leaped onto his back in fun or when I clutched them during orgasm.

I turned from the picture. Ruben shifted his gaze from Matt and looked down at me.

"He would have approved of this, us," I said. "He was a generous man." I shook my head. "Oh, I'm not saying he would have shared me while he was alive. He could get pretty jealous at times." I laughed, and Ruben gave a twitch of a smile. "Out of everyone, though, in the world, he would have wanted it to be you with me. I know that, in here." I pressed my fist to my chest. "It's only you, Ruben. You've pulled me from an abyss I just couldn't find my way out of — or ever thought I would."

He caught my face in his hands, closed his eyes and kissed me. He tasted of mint. I was sure I did, too, but there was so much more in our connection — trust, compassion, understanding, and what was the most thrilling of all, a future.

* * * *

"Wow, look at you!" Felicity exclaimed when I arrived at her parents' house. "You look bloody great, Katie."

"Thanks." I grinned and fiddled with the hem of my short, metallic-blue dress and glanced around the small living room packed full of glamorous girls. "Did you all know there's a white limo waiting outside?" I asked.

Felicity's eyes widened. "No, is there?" She dashed to the window, pulled back a net curtain and squealed. "Ah, there is. He's done it. I thought he was joking, but there actually *is* a limousine to take us to the club."

"God bless Neil Vickers," Melanie said, raising a glass of champagne into the air.

A whirlwind of activity followed — seven girls, all of whom I knew, gathering handbags and wraps. Then there was a great commotion of heels trapping across the wooden floor and into the hallway.

Felicity was last down the garden path. Her dress was shocking pink and barely covered the gusset of her knickers. She wore a veil that floated out behind her. On it someone, probably Melanie, had pinned condoms and tiny 'L' plates. She also had a smile on her face that could light up any dark room. Felicity had been in love with Neil for years, and finally she was about to get her man. Good for her.

We settled in the limousine. Sparkling wine flowed, and a beaty track started up as we pulled away from the curb.

"Seriously, you do look well," Felicity said, giving my knee a squeeze.

"I feel well. Northampton suits me." I smiled, a genuine one, the first these girls had seen me produce in a long time.

"It certainly does," Melanie said, touching my arm. "You have a glow about you."

I shrugged and sipped my drink.

"And you have a sparkle in your eye," Felicity said, studying me. She suddenly clasped her hand over her mouth, and her carefully plucked eyebrows stretched up into her forehead. "Have you?" she asked quietly.

I looked between her and Melanie, my two closest friends. "What do you mean?"

"Have you met someone?" Melanie asked.

"A bloke?" Felicity asked.

"Yes." I nodded, hesitant but thrilled to be saying it.

There was a flurry of hugs between the three of us.

"Give us details," Felicity said.

"No, it's your night. You don't want to hear about me."

She grasped my hand. "Nothing would make me happier tonight than to know things are starting to fall into place for you, Katie."

I sucked in a deep breath. "They are...really falling into place."

"What's his name?" Melanie asked.

"Ruben. Ruben Strong."

"Oh, and is he?" Felicity nudged me then flexed her arms, Popeye style.

I giggled. "Well, he works for me."

Melanie clinked her glass against mine then, "And how did you meet?"

These words had been rehearsed, and if I said them often enough I, too, would believe they were true. "I was wandering around the museum, you know, getting to know the place, and we got chatting."

"What, just started talking?"

"No, well, actually he saved me from a mad peacock that was trying to mug me."

"Wow, strong and brave." Felicity giggled.

"And kind and sweet and genuine and…" There were so many lovely words to describe Ruben. I could go on all night.

"I really am happy for you, Katie," Melanie said. "The new start, the move… Well, we were sad you left so suddenly and we miss you terribly, but to see you with a real smile? That makes it all worth it."

"Sure does," Felicity said. "And you absolutely must bring him to the wedding. I won't hear otherwise."

"Well, I'm not sure." Heck, was I ready to inflict this lot on Ruben? And could I stand amongst the friends that had only ever seen me with Matt and hold the hand of another man?

"You said it yourself," Felicity said. "He works for you, and in that case, he'll work for us too. I'll set him a place on the table plan."

"If you're sure." I worried at my bottom lip.

"As sure as I am of marrying Neil Vickers, that handsome, sexy devil." She kicked her legs in the air. "Whoohoo, soon I'm going to Mrs. Vickers and honeymooning in Spain. I'm going to have sex for breakfast, sex for lunch and sex for dinner, and I can't wait. I'm starving!"

I laughed along with everyone else. Her excitement about the future was infectious and there was a sudden lightness in her voice, an extra trill to her tone. I got the feeling she was more comfortable expressing her joy, knowing that I had some joy in my life too.

A true friend indeed.

* * * *

It had been gone noon by the time I'd left Melanie's house the day after the hen party. We'd spent the morning nursing our hangovers with a big fried breakfast and endless cups of tea. We'd had lots to talk about, not least Ruben and Northampton. She was impressed that I'd met Dean Cudditch and had confessed a secret crush.

After hugs and promises to stay in touch between now and the wedding, I'd headed to Matt's parents' house, a route I could do in my sleep.

I'd spent a couple of hours with them. Drank more tea and ate three freshly baked Eccles cakes. There was lots of talk of Matt, memories—happy ones mainly. It was soothing. It had made me feel like I wasn't the only one who missed him so terribly.

I'd known his parents had been to the deepest, blackest pits of hell too. But we'd gone our separate ways in grief. Them losing their child, despite him being an adult, was a bereavement that was profoundly different but no less intense than mine, and I hadn't felt we could offer each other much at a time neither of us had anything to give.

However, despite the ghost of Matt in the house— numerous school photographs, our wedding picture, his West Ham signed football on a stand in the hallway—they'd been well and had bought flowers for Matt's grave. They'd asked me to go with them to the cemetery, but I'd declined, wanting to give them their space. I'd go next time I was up, I'd promised, because there'd been one place drawing me stronger than anywhere else.

I stood now, beneath the arch of roses in St. Paul's churchyard. Morning congregation was long since over and there was no one around, just me and my memories.

The small pink flowers were in full bloom, and I let their powdery, perfumed scent fill my nose, as I closed my eyes and remembered another time and place, I smiled. For a second I was back there, Matt holding me, saying those words — till death do us part — then kissing me.

I didn't believe anyone had ever loved another person as much as I'd loved Matt right then. He had been my every breath, my dreams, my future — the one person who understood me. Our souls had been bound together by an invisible thread. From the moment I'd seen him across a busy pub, I'd known he was special. He'd said the same about me, and we'd always believed fate had been leading us up to that point in our lives. Ensuring circumstances had caused us to meet.

Opening my eyes, I blinked in the light of day and stroked my finger over the petals of one of the roses. If I hadn't moved to a flat, I would have planted more like these. They were my favorite. The baby pinkness of them so delicate and fragile, just like everything in life. Nothing was certain. It was good to remember that.

The church loomed before me. The tall bell tower stood silent and still, the sun beating down on its ancient stones. Sifting through recollections of our wedding day, I could still hear the wild clanking of the bells as we'd walked back down the aisle, my arm linked with his, a smile on my face so wide it had hurt my cheeks. They'd carried on ringing the bells while we'd had our pictures taken, but by the time we'd come back here, away from our guests for the private photograph, they'd stopped. Much like now, there'd been only the chatter of birds, the buzz of a bee and the rumble of a distant road.

I held up my left hand, looked at my bare ring finger and let the tears that were welling fall. They were allowed to. Today I was so sad, so heartbroken. I had to acknowledge that, live through it, because if I didn't it would eat me alive. My grief, as I'd discovered, was like a tumor. It kept on growing, stagnating, filling me up from the inside out. Pulling me between nausea and hopelessness.

But I'd found the cure. The cure was hope, a future, a new life. The cure was remembering Matt for the wonderful man and husband he had been and allowing myself to be happy again, or at least strive for that.

I wiped at the tears and sniffed. "I love you," I whispered to the roses above me. "Always—no matter what or who else I have in my life, I will always love you, Matt."

Chapter Twelve

Northampton was cast in shadows. A dull gray Monday that had brought drizzle to the park around the museum and thankfully sent the peacock searching for shelter—although that didn't stop me warily looking at the darkness beneath the enormous, leaf-heavy oak trees or glancing nervously in the direction of the aviary.

I wandered in through the open door of Ruben's workplace, the quiet stillness once again wrapping around me. This time the reception area didn't send my nerves skittering. Instead, it sent them jumping up and down with excitement and happy anticipation. I was looking forward to seeing Ruben. My morning had dragged as I'd counted the hours until we'd be together. The thought of lunch with him, having a look around the museum with him, hearing his voice, seeing his smile, had been like a crane lifting that damn weight out of my belly. It was a relief to see it go, to feel a lightness that allowed me to breathe.

The same lady as before sat at the leaflet-cluttered desk. Today she had on a navy fleece, and her name badge—*Ethel*—was pinned upside down. I smiled and walked up to the desk, decided not to tell her. It added to the charm of the place.

"Hello again," she said, shutting the thin paperback she was reading. "Have you come to see the rest of the museum?"

I was surprised she remembered me and smiled. "Yes, I…er… Ruben said he'd show me around."

She nodded seriously, the small red bead earrings she wore swinging in time with her movements. "I'm sure he did, a pretty girl like you."

I clasped my hands in front of me, glanced up the stairs. I'd hoped he'd be hanging about, waiting.

She smiled and her face softened. "He told me to expect you. Go straight up the stairs, through the Saints' room and then push through the door that says 'Staff Only'. His office is at the end. You'll see it."

"Okay, thanks." I touched my hair, hoping the breeze hadn't messed it up too much.

The museum was silent as I went up a level and walked through the first room. It was dedicated to the cobbling industry Northampton had been famous for. Old leather shoes in various states of disrepair were displayed in glass cabinets—none of them anything I'd want to wear.

The next room was exactly what Ethel had described, but not saints of the holy variety. This was the Saints rugby team, Northampton's pride and joy, and by the looks of the trophies and accolades, well worth that pride.

I spotted the 'Staff Only' door and pushed through it, feeling a smile already growing. The short corridor was empty, the walls a dull green, the carpet a faded orange. The door at the very end was ajar.

"Ruben?" I called, stepping toward it.

No answer.

I pushed it open. "Hey, there you are," I said.

He sat behind a dark wooden desk, a tired smile on his face, his arms folded in front of him.

"Shit, what's wrong?"

"Not feeling so great today."

"No kidding. You look bloody terrible." I dropped my bag on a tall-backed chair and rushed around the desk.

He straightened, as though stiff and aching, and swung his seat so he was facing me. His eyes were sunken, and he had mauve crescents beneath them. The rest of his face was pale and sallow.

I dropped to my knees, rested my hands on his legs. "You need to see a doctor."

"I'll be fine. It's probably just a cold."

"It's never just a cold for someone who's got a new heart, Ruben."

He shrugged, just a little.

"Seriously, I'm no medic, but even I know you need to see someone." I reached up, touched his cheek. He was clammy, and I didn't like it at all. "Have you got a specialist doctor you can ring?"

"Yeah, I suppose."

"So why didn't you?" Irritation snapped at my heels. "Ruben, you're sick. We need to get you better." He had to get better. I needed him.

"I might look like shit, but you look pretty," he said, squeezing my hand and giving me another one of his tired smiles.

Damn, I wanted to shake him. "Don't change the subject. Where is the number for your doctor?"

He sighed, as if defeated. "In here." He pulled out his wallet and plucked a business card from it. "I'll call him now."

"Yes, you do that." I stood, folded my arms, and resisted the urge to tap my foot. How could he have let himself get so ill? Didn't he know he was all I had? Didn't he understand Matt's heart was doing its best, but still, he had to take care of it?

A sudden thought hit me. What if it was my fault he was ill? Maybe it was that dash back from the cinema in the rain that had caused him to become sick? We'd gotten so wet, splashing through puddles and that car soaking us. That couldn't be good for him, surely.

"Hello, Andrew, it's Ruben Strong. Sorry to bother you." Ruben glanced at me, and I wanted to clip his ear for worrying about bothering his doctor when he looked like the gray day outside and was probably spiking a fever.

"Not so good actually. I think I've picked up a cold or a virus or something." There was a pause. "Yes, I increased them this morning when I first felt ill… Temperature, I think so."

I nibbled on a loose bit of skin by my thumbnail, watching Ruben doodle figures of eight on a notepad in front of him.

"I can be there in half an hour, yes. Thanks."

He clicked off the phone.

"Well?" I asked, touching his hair, stroking it back from his face and feeling terrible for being cross with him when he appeared completely drained of energy.

He looked up, his eyelids so heavy they were only half open. "He wants me to get to Northampton General. He's based in Oxford but he'll call and tell them to expect me and what drugs I need." He shrugged sadly. "It's happened a couple of times before."

I stooped and kissed his head. "Then come on. I'll drive you. I'm parked just outside."

He nodded.

"Can you walk that far?"

"Yes, don't fuss. I'll be fine." He set his jaw determinedly and stood.

"I'll go and get it then, drive it up to the front."

"Okay."

I grabbed my bag and dashed out of the door. Adrenaline spurred me on as I galloped past the Saints, the shoes then down the stairs.

"What's the rush?" Ethel asked, standing as I reached the bottom.

"He's ill. I've got to get him to hospital."

She put her hands beneath her chin as if in prayer. "Oh dear, I thought he seemed tired earlier, and here he's been…all morning up there, unwell. Oh dear…"

"It's all right." I touched her shoulder. "He's spoken to his doctor —"

"The heart one, the specialist?"

"Yes, and he needs some medication, as soon as possible."

Ethel started to walk left, changed her mind and walked right. "Oh dear," she said again.

"Listen, are you going to be able to lock up here? I don't want Ruben worrying about it."

"Yes, of course. I'll get the keys off him when he comes down." She shot a look up the stairs. "Oh dear."

"Yes, you do that, and I'll go and fetch my car."

* * * *

The bleeping of the cardiac monitor made me feel physically sick. The last time I'd heard that rhythmic sound I'd been holding Matt's hand and he'd been lying in intensive care. The ventilator had hissed and whirred at his side, his chest had moved up and down in synchrony with it.

He hadn't really been there, so they'd told me, but it had felt like it.

I clutched Ruben's hand the same way as I'd held Matt's, within both of mine, clasping it tight. He was asleep, had been for an hour, but I couldn't bear the thought of letting his hand go, of walking away from another man lying on a hospital bed and never seeing him again.

After the bustle of Ruben's arrival—an X-ray, blood tests and hooking him up to monitors and a drip—a young nurse had fluffed his pillow, taken his temperature again and told him that rest was the best thing now. He just needed to let the medicine do its job. She'd left the room then, shutting the door and leaving us alone.

I studied his sleeping face. He had more color since the oxygen tube had been placed beneath his nose. The grayness had gone, his lips pink again, their normal shade as opposed to whitish.

He was breathing steadily, and his skin, although still a fraction too warm, had lost the clamminess from earlier. The bed sheets were rolled down to his waist, and I set my attention on his scar and thought of his new heart pounding away, working its hardest to do its job, even though Ruben's body saw it as an invader.

Weariness suddenly took over me. I couldn't imagine going home to sleep, so I rested my head on the bed, next to our joined hands, and shut my eyes.

I must have slept for a while, because when the click of the door woke me, the shadows in the room had stretched and the sun had come out, creating a diamond shape on the wall behind Ruben's bed.

"Oh, I'm very sorry, I…didn't realize."

I turned at the sound of a female voice. Standing in the doorway was a middle-aged couple. They were both tall—she had her hair in a neat, pale blonde bob and his was gray and short.

I cleared my throat, sat up straighter, kept Ruben's hand in both of mine.

"Er, hello," I said.

The couple continued to stare at me.

I glanced at Ruben. He was snoring softly.

"How is he?" the man asked, stepping into the room. He had the same soft brown eyes as Ruben and moved in a similar, long-limbed way.

"He just needs to wait for the medicines to work and then he'll feel fine," I said. "So the doctor told us."

"Well, that sounds encouraging." He smiled. "I'm Trevor, Ruben's father."

"Hello, nice to meet you. I'm Katie."

"And this is my wife, Veronica, his mother."

Veronica Strong crossed the room. She was elegant in neat trousers, a pale blue blouse and a string of pearls that had been wrapped twice around her neck.

"Hello," I said.

She smiled but only briefly, because then she took Ruben's other hand in hers, being careful of the drip, and studied him. Her whole posture projected worry and fear. She nibbled on her bottom lip and frowned.

"When did he get ill?" she asked.

"I saw him at lunchtime. He said he'd been feeling under the weather since this morning."

"Well, at least he caught it quickly this time. He can be so stubborn."

"I made him call the doctor."

"Good. Thank you."

I nodded.

She let her gaze roam over me, frowned slightly. "I didn't know he was seeing anyone," she said. "I thought he would have mentioned it—"

"Veronica," Trevor said.

She turned her mouth down and shook her head. "I'm sorry. That was rude of me." She looked at Ruben again.

"It's okay—us, Ruben and I—it's all been a bit of a whirlwind. We got close fast." I paused, thought how deeply he'd gotten under my skin. "Happens like that sometimes, doesn't it?"

"I suppose so." She glanced at me again, slightly suspiciously.

"Hey, Mum, Dad," Ruben said in a croaky voice. "You got the message I left you, then."

"Yes, we came straight here," Veronica said. "How are you feeling?"

"Not so bad. Been worse."

"Well, we know that, son," Trevor said, putting a pile of magazines on the table at the end of the bed, all motor related. "The thing is, how long are you planning on being in here instead of out courting this beautiful lady?"

Ruben smiled at his father then at me. "This is Katie," he said. "Sorry. I should have introduced you."

"We've done that already," Veronica said. "But you didn't mention Katie when I spoke to you yesterday."

"No, well, we're still getting used to there being an us, aren't we?" He turned his hand over and took hold of mine, instead of me holding his.

"Yes," I said with a smile. "You look better now than you did earlier."

"I feel it. Thanks for driving me here."

"As if you need to say thanks."

Veronica picked up a glass of water. "You should drink," she said to Ruben.

He let go of my hand, drank as instructed.

"Have you eaten?" he said to me then turned to his mother. "We we're going for lunch. We never made it."

"No, I'm not hungry."

"You have to eat, Katie." He frowned at me.

"I will, later."

"I could murder a cup of tea after the drive here," Veronica said. "Come on, Katie. Let's go to the canteen together."

She and Ruben both held the same determined expression, the same set to their jaws, the same sure look in their eyes. I could refuse, stamp my feet and demand that I not be told what to do. But I couldn't be bothered. My emotional energy was running on low today, and a cup of tea was tempting.

"Yes, you ladies go and chatter. I need the inside gossip about the race on Saturday," Trevor said, tapping the side of his nose. "And no doubt it'll be juicy if Dean Cudditch has anything to do with it."

Ruben laughed, and the sound settled in my chest like a tonic.

"Of course it is," he said. "Dean is always flying by the seat of his pants."

* * * *

Ten minutes later, I was nursing a cup of tea and an egg-and-cress sandwich bought for me, with much insistence, by Veronica.

She plucked a tub of sweeteners from her handbag, added one to her tea then stirred. I looked at the enormous rock on her left ring finger alongside a thick gold band then glanced at my bare one.

"So how did you two meet?" she asked, smiling stiffly.

"I was wandering around the museum and we got chatting."

She nodded, took a sip of tea.

"He saved me from a peacock. It was trying to attack me."

She smiled. "Really, that's quite a way to meet."

"I suppose."

"Why don't you eat, Katie? You don't look like you can afford to lose weight."

I resisted responding with a sharp comment and tore the cellophane off the wrapped sandwich.

"And are you from around here?"

I held back a sigh. This was going to be a serious grilling. But what the hell, Ruben, like Matt had been to his mother, was clearly the light of her life. Heck, he was the light in mine now, so we shared a common interest. I'd give her what she wanted. Well, most of it.

"No, I'm born and raised in Yorkshire. I moved here from Leicester, where I'd been working for several years. I needed a change."

"Oh, had something gone wrong in Leicester?"

"No, I just wanted to transfer jobs. I work at Skin Deep, in town."

"Oh, yes, very nice."

I picked up a sandwich, nibbled the corner. "It is nice. The staff are friendly and I like the products, plus it's very convenient."

"For what?"

"I mean…it's low stress, that suits me."

She raised her eyebrows.

I took a proper bite of sandwich, studied the iridescent sheen on her pearls, then when I'd swallowed said, "I've never been a career girl, no wild ambitions to climb the dizzy heights of the corporate ladder and change the world."

"Oh, that's unusual these days. I thought all you young ladies were ready to take on anything."

"Not me."

She tipped her head, urging me to go on.

I braced, steadying myself on the wire, an invisible balancing pole in my hands keeping me on the straight and narrow and leaving the hurricane of emotions down below. "I fell in love, Mrs. Strong, when I was young. We got married, Matt and I. We settled down, planned a family—a boy and a girl. I wanted to be a mother, a wife, a friend, a lover. I was so close to having all of those things, but then one day everything changed."

I had her attention now. Her mask had slipped. She wasn't being the suspicious, protective parent anymore. She was curious. She wanted to know what had happened to me. Did she imagine I'd run away and left my family? Maybe she thought I'd become a druggie or an alcoholic and they'd all left me. Maybe I'd committed some horrible crime and been locked up at Her Majesty's pleasure for the last few years.

"What changed?" she asked quietly.

I set the sandwich aside. "He died, my husband. He was killed in an accident, and my life was turned upside down." My voice broke on the last word, but I held it together. Disguised it well, I hoped.

Instantly she reached out and placed her hand on mine. "I'm sorry."

I nodded. Would she still be sorry if she knew my husband's death had saved her son? Would she still regret my loss? What if she could turn the clock back for Matt, would she save him?

What-ifs served no use. I'd learned that as sure as I'd learned the earth kept spinning. What-ifs had tortured me to no avail.

"It was hard," I said. "Grief is a persistent beast that takes a long time to fight. Beating it is impossible, learning to live with it the best you can do."

"It's not a pleasant path to walk or even consider walking." She removed her hand and curled it around her cup. "Has Ruben told you his history?"

I nodded. "Yes."

"All of it?"

"I think so."

"He nearly died, too, you know?"

"Because of his heart?"

"Yes. His illness made him very sick. He became half the man he was, less even."

"That must have been horrible to see."

"Agony for his father and me. He was literally slipping away before our very eyes, and there was nothing we could do but hope for a miracle."

"Miracles are in short supply."

"Yes, but we were lucky. We were blessed with one."

I'd given them their miracle. I could have said no to the organ retrieval team, because it had been up to me — my decision entirely — no persuasion, no convincing. But I hadn't said no. In the foggy corners of my agonized brain, I'd dredged up the answer yes.

"The heart Ruben has in his chest now." She paused. "It's a new one. His lungs too, for that matter. He had a transplant."

"Yes, he told me."

She breathed out. "Good, I'm glad." She touched her pearls. "He doesn't tell many people, Katie. I don't know why. Maybe it's a male pride thing."

"I think that's exactly it. What bloke wants a girl to feel sorry for him or think he's not as tough as he looks?"

She leaned forward. "He is, though—tough, that is. What he went through, most people would have begged to be put out of their misery. But not my son, he had this fight for life, this will to live that staggered even the medical staff at times."

"I can imagine."

"If you know him at all, then yes, you probably can." She dropped the pearls she was fiddling with, balled her hands into fists on the table. "Katie, I want you to understand what you're getting involved with. My son is just returning to the land of the living. He hasn't dated for a long time, and I know he hankers after his old life of fast cars and traveling the world. I'm not sure if that will ever happen again for him, so he needs something to replace that. He has a future now, thanks to our miracle, but he has to have a reason for getting up each morning."

"Mrs. Strong, with all due respect, I think we're both just finding our feet after a really crap time. Safety in numbers—doing it together—is working out pretty well so far, although he scared the living daylights out of me today."

She sighed. "He's done this a few times since the transplant—he'll be okay, though. The drugs just need to be blasted into him for twenty-four hours. But of course, catching it early has helped."

"Yes." I stared at my tea, the brown puddle that it was, sitting in the pure-white cup. Silence stretched between us. I didn't like to say that us getting wet and tumbling into bed still soaking might have something to do with his illness. But it wasn't, surely.

"I guess what I'm really trying to say is…" Veronica said, snapping me from my self-blame.

"What?"

She touched her hair then placed her hand on her chest. "Please be gentle with him. He's been through so much." She paused, seemed to summon up the courage to speak again. "Please, just don't break his heart. It's delicate in more ways than one."

I touched the hand she still had resting on the table, cupped my palm over her knuckles. "Don't worry. His new heart is very precious to me. I won't do anything to hurt it, ever."

Chapter Thirteen

"Oh my goodness, I swear that one is a Marshmallow Man." I pointed out of the window and laughed. I'd never seen anything like it.

"Where?" Ruben looked, saw the hot-air balloon I was flapping my hand at and chuckled. "It looks like the one from Ghostbusters."

The sky from Ruben's flat—he had an amazing view of the park, which meant the festival too—was a multicolored sea of inflated balloons, but few were traditional shapes. The majority were novelty, and I marveled at how some could fly. They were so big.

"This is crazy." I sat back on his sofa that we'd spun to face the window. It was like having our own private box. Down below, people milled about—kids eating candyfloss, toddlers in buggies pointing excitedly, couples strolling hand in hand. A carousel and a big wheel had been set up. Music and laughter and the *whoosh* of flames lifting the balloons from the ground breezed through the open window.

"More wine?" Ruben asked.

"No, I'm fine." I set my glass on the table.

We'd enjoyed our own indoor picnic. Not because Ruben wasn't well or that we didn't fancy mooching around the festival, but because we could enjoy it from the comfort of his home and that was a unique experience.

"Last year they had a McLaren balloon, shaped like a Formula One car. It was huge, probably the biggest, and I think it went the fastest too."

"Why does that not surprise me?"

He reached for my hand, kissed my knuckles. "I would have organized for us to go up in one if you'd wanted to."

"No, I don't think I could cope with that. I like my feet firmly on the floor."

"Of course." He put his arm around me.

I snuggled in close, loving his body against mine. He'd only spent forty-eight hours in hospital, and had been back at work the next week. His strength had returned quickly, and we'd been spending as much time as possible together. Enjoying our new romance and the closeness that went with it. We'd both had enough of battling on alone.

"Next weekend," I said, tracing my finger over his belly, rucking his T-shirt as I went, "my friend Felicity is getting married."

"The girl whose hen night you went to?"

"Yes, that's right. Well, I told her about you and…" I paused. "I don't know if you're up for it, but she wants you to come to the wedding. With me, as my guest."

"And that makes you nervous."

I looked up at him, stilled my finger. "A little."

"Because they've only ever seen you with Matt?"

How did he just get that? I didn't know, but I was grateful he did and I didn't need to spell it out for him. "Yes."

"Well, you could always make up some excuse for me. Say I'm off bungee jumping that weekend or something."

"No, I want you there. I don't want to spend the weekend without you, and besides, Matt's gone. It's us now, Katie and Ruben."

"Yes." He stroked my cheek. "It's us now."

"I want everyone to know it."

"Me too." He smiled.

"So you'll come?"

"Absolutely. And I'll be on my best behavior."

I rolled my eyes. "Right, because the girls are always *so* well behaved."

"What I mean is, I won't do any of this."

Suddenly I was on my back and he was over me. I giggled and wrapped my arms around his neck, my legs around his thighs. "I should think not, Mr. Strong, and certainly not in church."

"Mmm, but later, at the reception." He pressed a kiss to my lips. He tasted of wine and the salty crisps we'd been eating. "In our hotel room, maybe, then I'll have my wicked way with you and do all the things I've been dreaming of doing."

"I've unleashed a monster," I said with a smile then groaned when the hardness of his cock, through our jeans, surged against my mound.

"You really want to see my monster?"

"I think I'd better. See if it can ever be tamed."

He kissed me again, slanting his head and probing deep. He swept his hand up the inside of my T-shirt, squeezed my breast then tweaked my nipple through my thin bra.

I became lost in him. Every sense was focused on Ruben. A hungry need settled between my legs.

"I want you now," he whispered hotly. "Here."

We'd made love several times since he'd left hospital, but in bed, at my place, quiet, slow, intense, the same as the first time. I wasn't complaining. It was wonderful, but this was new. This was middle-of-the-day sex, and damn, I wanted some.

"Yes," I said, "fuck me."

He raised his head, stared down at me. A devilish smile curled his lips. "Say that again."

"What?" I pushed his flopping hair back from his forehead.

"What you just asked me to do."

Ah, he likes dirty talk. I can do that. "Fuck me, Ruben. Fuck me now. Make me come. Make me scream your name."

"Oh, Jesus." His mouth went slack. "Get naked." He reached for his top, yanked it off, his face now a picture of urgency.

I did the same with my T-shirt, wriggling on the sofa then tossing the material aside.

He dipped his head to my chest, tugging at my bra.

"Oi! Get a room!" shouted a deep, bellowing but distanced voice through the window.

We both froze.

"Shit," Ruben said, screening my body with his. "What the...?"

I looked outside. Not thirty feet from the flat was a huge basket with two men in it. A massive flame burned bright behind them, sending an orange glow over their bodies. They wore flat caps but didn't look particularly old—one had a black mustache, the other was holding a rope.

"I have got a bloody room," Ruben shouted. "Bugger off!"

The men laughed, the flame burned brighter and they started to lift upward.

"Have fun," the one with the mustache called with a wave.

"We will," I shouted, managing to wave back as they went from view.

Ruben looked down at me. "I'm really sorry about that. I had no idea they'd come so close."

I swatted his shoulder and smiled. "It was funny. They couldn't believe their eyes. They thought they were going to see some action."

"Pervs." Ruben grinned. "Now, where were we?"

"You were just about to fuck me."

"Damn, you have such a filthy mouth."

"And don't you know it."

"Not as much as I'd like to." He unclipped my bra, sat up and squeezed my breasts together, his thumbs toying with my nipples.

I arched into him, loving the sensation of him touching me and gazing so adoringly at me. "So how about I tell you to get your cock out," I said, reaching for his waistband. "Get it out and show me what you can do with it."

"So sweet, yet so dirty." He smirked. "But hang on." He stood, went to the window and drew the curtains. "Just in case we have any more voyeurs. I don't want them seeing what I'm about to do with my cock."

"I like the sound of that." I licked my lips.

"Do you now?"

He looked tall and hot standing over me and slowly undoing the buttons on his jeans—long arms and legs, strong fingers, the perfect spread of body hair and an air of absolute determination about him.

"You'd best take your trousers off or they might get ripped," he said, nodding at my jeans.

"Yes, sir. Whatever you say, sir."

He rolled his eyes, groaned. "Now you're just messing with my head, woman."

I giggled, sat and shoved off my jeans. "I can mess with any bit of you that needs dirtying up."

"Will this do for starters?" He fisted his cock, moved toward me and slotted one hand in my hair.

Sat on the sofa, I was the perfect height to take him into my mouth.

"As long as I still get the main course," I said.

"You can count on that."

I eyed the slit at the end of his dick—dark and deep. My mouth watered for the flavor of him. He held me tight, and I opened up to take what he offered.

"Ah, yeah, that's so hot to watch." He groaned as he sank in.

My heart was tripping. This was a new side to Ruben, more dominant, more assertive. I liked it, a lot. I could be his to do whatever he desired with. It would suit me very much. I just wanted to make him happy, and I knew full well he'd make me happy.

He set up a steady rhythm, fucking my mouth. I held his root with one hand, applying firm pressure, and slid the other round to clutch at his tight bum.

His cock swelled. A drip of pre-cum coated my tongue. His breaths grew faster, several moans released on exhales.

"Stop," he said, pulling out. "Or it will be over too early."

My mouth felt empty. I looked up and pouted.

"Don't give me that look," he said.

"I was having fun."

"Me too, too much fun." He wrapped his hand around his cock. "Besides, I thought you wanted me to fuck you."

"I do. I want you to fuck me hard and fast and not to stop until your balls feel like they're coming out of the end of your cock."

His mouth dropped open, his eyes widened, and he shook his head. "And here was my parents saying what a lovely, charming girl you are."

"Sod charming." I knew he was loving my filthy words. His eyes were bright. His cock looked ready to explode. I sat back, pushed off my knickers and spread my legs. "Give it to me, big boy."

He stared at my pussy. "Fuck, I'm the luckiest man on Earth."

"You'd better believe it."

He was over me again, and we were flat on the sofa. In one sharp thrust he pounded into me.

I cried out. The speed of him—he was so hard—it was a stitch of pain but also wonderful.

"Sorry. Are you all right?"

I thumped his shoulder with my fist. "Yes, oh, don't stop. Give it to me like that, Ruben. That's it."

It was as though I'd flicked a switch in him. He withdrew then powered back in, shunting me up the cushions. I clung to him and canted my pelvis to get maximum connection against my clit.

"Ah, yeah, I'm fucking you now. Is that how you want it?" he said into my ear.

His deliciously sinful words nearly pushed me over the edge. "Yes, oh, yes, take me. I'm yours."

If I thought we'd been wild before, now we cranked up a level. Ruben was no longer the mild, gentle lover he had been. He was throwing solid male muscle behind each thrust as he blasted his dick into me.

I couldn't control my breaths as our chests banged together. I didn't try to, I just let the air huff and groan from me. It felt so good, the pressure mounting so fast. I shut my eyes, absorbed everything about him—his scent, the feel of his skin and body hair against my chest and belly, the way his breaths were also erratic and thundering into my ear and down my neck.

"Ah, ah, I'm coming…" he gasped.

"Me too. Oh, don't stop." I dragged my nails down his back, gripped his legs with my ankles and pushed up to meet his thrusts.

"Fuck…ah, yes." He intensified his hold around my shoulders, held me so tight my ribs could hardly expand. "Come, baby. Come with me."

"Yes, yes…"

I let the power of my climax seize me, throw me every which way, hanging on to Ruben for support so I didn't lose myself completely. I was aware of his deep, guttural groan in my ear and let it swirl with my own moan of ecstasy. We were holding nothing back. Our pleasure, physical, vocal and emotional, was all out there to be celebrated. The ride was spectacular, and I pulsed through my orgasm, completely surrendered to Ruben and the exquisite sensations owning my body.

He slowed his frantic pace, lifted his head and stared down at me. His hair was mussed and his eyes sparkled. "My God, that was amazing."

"Tell me about it," I said breathlessly then shivered as my pussy contracted around his cock in another orgasmic tremor. "Ah, yeah." I let my eyes roll back in their sockets. "So amazing."

He ground into me one last time, and I wrapped my arms around his neck as our mouths connected. I was hot and tingling. Being held so tightly and kissed so sweetly made me feel as if everything would be all right forever.

Eventually he broke the kiss and withdrew his softening cock. "We got a bit wild there," he said, looking down at my naked body that was red from friction, damp from sweat.

"I think it was the dirty talk that unleashed the beast." I giggled.

"Damn, I'd forgotten how much I liked a pretty girl with a gutter mouth."

I drew my legs together but stayed flat on the sofa, my body heavy and suddenly weary. "I don't usually, only in the bedroom."

"Or living room." He smiled and reached for his boxers.

I enjoyed the view of his bum as he bent over. "Oh, bugger," I said when he straightened. "Your back." He had several long, red scratches across his shoulder blades.

He pulled up his underwear and twisted his neck. "What?"

"I'm afraid I've…" I waved my finger at him. "Left my mark."

He grinned. "And I'll wear it with pride." He touched his lips to mine. "Do you want a drink?"

"Mmm." I stretched my arms over my head, squirmed lazily. "A cup of tea would be lovely."

"Coming right up."

I shut my eyes and listened to Ruben moving around the kitchen. The breeze seeping beneath the curtains was a lick of cool on my hot, naked body, and I sighed and let contentment weave deeper into my soul than it had in a long time.

The noise of the festival mixed in with my easy thoughts, as did the first rumbles of the kettle. My mind flashed back to Ruben's face when I'd asked him to fuck me, and a smile balled my cheeks. That was a moment in time I'd come back to over and over.

Soon my contemplations overtook the sounds around me. My body was heavy, slumber had stolen me. I let myself drift into a dreamy world.

* * * *

Kisses as soft as kitten's whiskers trickled up my belly, fluttering, floating, spreading into the dip of my waist and onto the curve of my breast. I sighed and squirmed, just a little, inviting more of the blissful sensations.

A fingertip meandered down my side, from just below my breast into the indent of my navel. So light it was barely a caress, so gentle it was hardly there. It tickled, but in a good way, and I smiled and turned my head on the cushion.

A sudden panic gripped me, like a fist around my heart. Damn, it was happening again. I was alone. There was no one kissing me. I'd wake up any second and that weight would plunge me to the bottom of the cold, dark ocean of grief.

I gasped, clenched my fists.

"Your tea is getting cold, sleepyhead."

I opened my eyes. Stared at the checked pattern on Ruben's curtains then down at his face. He was peppering kisses on my belly, just to the right of my navel.

"I found a bit I hadn't kissed," he said with a soft smile. "I felt it important to rectify the situation."

I touched his face and felt his stubble on my palm. I ran my other hand through his hair, letting it drift through my fingers. Ruben was here. I wasn't alone. Those kisses were real.

Ruben was real.

I dragged in a deep breath. Fear was a powerful thing, and it took an even stronger emotion to beat it into submission.

Love.

I realized then, in that moment, that I was head-over-heels in love with Ruben. There was no question about it. I wanted him, needed him. He'd become my everything, and I wanted it to stay that way.

"Shall I pass your tea?" he asked, seemingly satisfied that he'd kissed the neglected square inch of my flesh sufficiently.

The curtains shifted, creating a slash of daylight across the room. His face came into bright sunlight. He squinted, and slanted his head, shifting the shadows angled on his face.

The face I now wanted to start and end my days with. And if I didn't? Goodness only knew what would be left of me.

Chapter Fourteen

"We'll be late," I said, glancing at the clock. "We only have fifteen minutes until it starts."

"It'll be fine," Ruben said, looking in the mirror and doing up his tie. "It's not like we have to go anywhere now that we're finally here. They're getting married in this hotel."

"I suppose." I slipped my feet into high, silver sandals then straightened my dress. "Can you do me up?"

I turned, and he reached for the zipper and tugged. As he did so, the pale lilac dress hugged me, the silky lining pressing against my flesh.

"You look very pretty," he said when I studied myself in the mirror.

"Do you think?"

"Yes, perfect." He touched his lips to my hair then he, too, glanced at the clock. "Shame we really, really have to go."

I smiled and ran my hands over my hips. I'd put on some weight. I was sure of it. I filled the dress out much better than when I'd worn it several months ago to a christening. Not loads of weight, but there wasn't a gap between the neckline and my breasts now, and my hips had a hint of curve to them that had been lacking for so long. I touched my hair, carefully pinned in a twist on the crown of my head then happy with my finished look, I grabbed my clutch. "Let's go."

Ruben snapped down the hem of his suit jacket, straightened the cuffs then scooped up the room key. He hesitated.

"What's up?" I asked.

He frowned, looked down at himself. "Will I do?"

"You look very smart. That new suit fits you lovely."

He fiddled with his red paisley tie again. It had been perfectly straight but he'd knocked it to the left.

I went up to him, re-aligned it. "You look smart and gorgeous, and I can't wait to show you off."

"Really?"

"Yes, really." I touched my lips to his.

He pulled in a breath. "We'd best get going then."

"Yes, we don't want to be the last in."

We walked across the hotel foyer toward the orangery where Felicity and Neil's ceremony was to be held. I slotted my hand through the crook of Ruben's arm.

"This is a seriously nice place," Ruben said before letting out a low whistle.

"Mmm, very posh. Must have cost a fortune to hire."

Grand marble pillars supported an ornate ceiling, gigantic bunches of flowers were set on the long reception desk, and staff in neat navy suits and peaked caps were discreetly going about their business.

A white sign on a stand directed wedding guests to the orangery. As we approached the glass-paned doors, the tinkle of gentle music grew louder.

I steeled myself, not because I was nervous of seeing my friends or that I wasn't beyond proud to have Ruben at my side, but just because he wasn't Matt. All social events, up to this point in my life, I'd always been with Matt or alone these last two years, but now that had changed.

My friends were happy for me. I knew that. This was good change, but still...happiness lined with sadness was a complex maze to navigate. I would do the best I could and hope that I didn't bang up against too many dead ends.

We went into the beautiful, sunny orangery. Lemon-colored flowers had been arranged on huge pedestals in each corner and at the front of the aisle. The white seats had big yellow bows on the backs of them. Most were filled, and people were chatting quietly amongst themselves. Neil and his best man were talking to the registrar. Due to heavy motorway traffic, we'd arrived at the hotel with only minutes to spare before the bride made her entrance.

I spotted Melanie, halfway down. She turned, as if sensing me there, and gestured.

"Melanie has saved us seats," I said to Ruben. "Look." I stepped ahead of him, felt his hand on the small of my back.

Melanie stood and kissed my cheek. "You look fabulous," she said.

"Thanks," I turned. "This is Ruben Strong."

Ruben held out his hand, but Melanie ignored it and planted a kiss on his cheek. "Hello, Ruben," she said. "I've heard all about you."

"All good, I hope."

"Oh, yes, all very good indeed." She smiled and gestured to her boyfriend of several years. "This is Andy."

Andy shook Ruben's hand, too, and I gave him a kiss. He was quiet and easy-going. I'd always presumed he just liked Melanie's efficiency and was happy to go along with whatever she organized.

We took our seats, and I waved hello at several other friends, all of whom were casting sneaky glances at Ruben. And why not? He looked incredibly handsome. If I'd seen him across a room, I, too, would have a second, third and fourth look.

He was winding his thumbs around each other, so I took his hand, squeezed gently. "Felicity has been dreaming of this day for years," I said. "It took Neil a while to get around to popping the question but once he did, that was it. She was a force to be reckoned with when it came to planning this day."

"It has a nice feel to it." He nodded at the huge expanse of glass that domed out into the manicured gardens of the hotel. "It's light and airy. The outside coming in."

"Yes, and—"

I stopped talking as the bridal march rang around the room. The congregation stood, and I turned and strained my neck to see Felicity walking down the aisle with her father.

Wearing a figure-hugging gown and a veil—thankfully minus the condoms—that trailed on the floor behind her, she looked stunning. She held a bouquet of citrus blooms and wore a diamond necklace that sparkled in the streaming sunshine.

A tingle ran over my spine and diffused across my shoulders. My own memory of walking down the aisle and seeing Matt turn and smile hovered in my mind's eye.

I'd been so happy, flying high. It had been a wonderful moment in my life. One I would cherish forever.

Ruben's shoulder rubbed mine as he picked up the order of service and passed me a copy. I looked up at him and saw that he was studying me with concern on his face. He knew me so well. He was wondering if I was okay with this whole wedding thing.

I smiled, nodded and the crease between his eyebrows softened. Because I *was* all right, I had my balance, and this particular part of the maze had shown me the way.

And the way forward was the present. Enjoying Felicity and Neil's special moment, with Ruben at my side in this beautiful place surrounded by friends was my new path.

The past was allowed to ripple up my back, touch my shoulder or stroke my cheek. That was fine, but what I wanted most was to hold hands with the future. It was the only way to step forward.

* * * *

The ceremony went without a hitch. After a ton of photographs on the lawn and the release of two white doves that promptly flew up into the nearest tree and started mating, we were all herded into a lavishly decorated reception room.

Ruben and I were seated with Melanie and Andy, along with a couple of other girls I knew through Felicity.

The conversation flowed, only pausing for the formal speeches and the cutting of the cake. Ruben held his own when teased by Melanie for his sideburns that suited him very well, and I caught up with Lauren about her baby girl whose christening I'd attended.

It seemed hardly no time had passed when the plates were cleared away and the disco music started.

"Please all circle the floor for the first dance," the DJ called through his microphone.

Ruben took my hand, and we wandered to the outer rim of the large rectangular dance floor. Red, yellow and blue spotlights spun around us as the first bars of an old, haunting U2 song, *With or Without You*, strummed out.

The crowd around us increased as Felicity and Neil embraced and began to sway to the music, eyes only for each other. Ruben slipped behind me to make room for someone smaller than him to see.

The bass guitar rumbled through my chest, its rhythm as familiar as a heartbeat. This had been Matt's favorite song out of all the U2 ones he'd adored. I remembered sitting on his shoulders when it had played at the first concert he'd taken me to.

"Who sings this?" Ruben asked, winding his arms around my waist and pulling my back into his chest.

I tilted my chin and twisted to reply. "U2. It's really old, though."

"It's good. I don't know much of their stuff. I'm more of a Coldplay and Oasis kind of guy, but this…"

"You should get into them. I've got all of their music."

"Can I borrow it?"

"Sure."

He touched his lips to my temple, and as I listened to the song, I melted into him, his support welcomed. I was glad of the darkness, though. The words, living with or without someone, had created a ripple effect on my tightrope. It was as if someone had given it a twang and it took all my effort to stay steady.

I watched Felicity turn her head and smile at something Neil was whispering in her ear. A new memory for them, a perfect moment. I made it one of mine, too, and solidified my emotional stability.

The song came to an end, and I found myself tugged farther onto the dance floor. "Time for *our* first dance," Ruben said, gathering me close.

I slipped my hands over his shoulders and linked my fingers at his nape. "And a perfect song for us," I said, smiling as The Police started up with *Every Breath You Take*.

"Mmm." He touched his lips to mine and planted several delicate kisses that made me fall into him all the more. Ruben's taste, the way he made me feel, his arms around me, was like an addiction. Luckily it seemed he felt the same way about me and we were happy to feed each other what we needed.

He tucked a loose tendril of hair behind my ear, spun me one-eighty, and I smiled up at him.

"You're doing so well, today," he said.

"What do you mean?"

"A wedding, it must be hard not to think of your own."

"Yes, it is. But I have you here, and the difference that's made is incredible. I feel like Katie around my friends again. I'm not sad and lonely and trying to cover it up with fake smiles. They can see that I'm happy and they don't need to feel guilty for their own happiness. Does that make sense?"

"Yes, it's like a domino effect when people feel sorry for you. The brighter you try and be, the more sympathy they project, which in turn makes you feel worse inside."

I loved it that he understood me so well. It made everything so much simpler. "That's right." I slid my hands down from his shoulders, settled them on his chest.

He took my left one in his. "Do you think you ever would again?" he asked.

"What do you mean?"

"Get married."

"I've never thought about it." I'd thought about a future with Ruben, but marriage? "Why? Are you asking?" I smiled.

"Let's just say I'm dipping my toe into the marriage pond to see what the temperature is."

I laughed. "That's a really silly analogy."

He grinned. "But it made you laugh and that's what thrills me the most." He pressed our joined hands into his chest, over his heart. "But seriously, Katie. A minute without you is a wasted minute, and I, for one, know time should never be wasted."

"I feel the same," I said, looking into his eyes that were reflecting the fragments of bright lights bouncing around us.

"So we should do something about that."

"What are you suggesting?"

"Move in with me. My flat is big enough for the two of us. I want to wake up with you every morning, go to sleep with you in my arms every night. It just makes so much sense to be together."

I'd been moving gently to the music but stopped. "Really? Are you serious?"

"Absolutely. I'm in love with you, Katie, and I can't bear to be apart from you. You've completely stolen my heart."

"And you mine," I said, curling my hand around the back of his head and pulling him closer. "I'm so in love with you," I breathed onto his mouth. "And yes, I want you to be the first person I see each morning and the one I kiss goodnight."

"So that's a yes?" He gave a tentative smile.

"Oh, yes, a big fat yes with icing and cherries on the top."

We kissed, in front of all of my friends, people who'd seen me with another man on my wedding day, seen me become a shell of myself after his death and now rise from the flames like a phoenix. I was so happy I wanted to burst with joy.

But I'd settle for getting naked and sweaty.

Chapter Fifteen

We fell into our hotel room. Ruben kicked the door shut and dropped the key to the floor. Next thing I knew I was up against the wall, my wrists held above me in just one of his hands. He was staring down at me, his nostrils flaring as he breathed fast.

"Tell me this is it," he said, palming my left breast through my dress with his free hand.

"Yes, this is it," I panted.

"You and me?"

"Yes, you and me."

He smiled, not in his usual sweet way but in a downright predatory way. "And what do you want?"

Excitement and anticipation swirled in my belly. Between my legs I was buzzing for attention. "You, Ruben. Fuck me. I want you to fuck me."

He gritted his teeth, but only briefly because then he caught my mouth in a wild kiss.

I pushed against him as he drove me harder into the wall with his body. There was nothing weak about him. He had me held tight with his chest, his belly and legs all taut with muscle and his lust as powerful as any force I'd ever known.

I matched him kiss for kiss, looped my right leg around one of his. Tried to move my arms but couldn't.

"Like this," he said, suddenly releasing me and spinning me to face the long mirror next to us. "Bend over. Put your arms out."

I stooped and pressed my palms onto the cool surface. He yanked my short dress up to my waist and tugged my knickers off. Cool air washed over my bum and legs.

His movements were swift, precise and within seconds, his cock was nudging at my pussy from behind.

Spreading my legs to make his entry easier, I watched in the mirror as he concentrated on his task, his hair flopping forward and his tie hanging loose, tapping against the small of my back.

But he didn't penetrate me with his cock. Instead, he plunged two fingers into my pussy.

I shunted forward and gasped, the filling as sweet as it was intense.

"So wet for me," he said, withdrawing then pushing back in, just teasing my G-spot the way he was so damn expert at. "You're perfect for me."

I forced myself to continue watching his reflection. He was tall and wide, looming behind me. Still wearing his suit it seemed extra sexy, extra forbidden that we'd snuck away from the celebrations to satisfy our sudden carnal urges.

"I'll never get enough of you," he said, fingering me, "or your sexy pussy."

"Mmm...oh yes...but..." I needed more stimulation so let go of the mirror and searched out my clit.

"Oh, no you don't," he said, pushing me away, "that's my job." He took over with his free hand, working and rubbing, building me up.

I locked my knees and whimpered a complaint when he removed his fingers but then braced as he pushed his cock into me that first inch.

He gripped my left hip, kept working my clit. "I'm in heaven when I'm in you," he said, sinking balls deep, and a long, low grunt of pleasure erupting from him.

"Me too," I gasped. "When you're in me."

Palms still on the mirror, I took him all, so deep he nudged right up to my cervix. I adored this position, I'd forgotten how much, and being able to see the bliss on his face as he withdrew then thrust back in was sublime.

He held me tight. I was a little unstable, my concentration wavering from my legs to my pussy. An orgasm was blooming. His fingers were wicked, unrelenting, feeding a pressure in my clit that was demanding more, more, more.

"Ruben," I gasped. "Oh, God."

I didn't know how I managed to stay on my feet as the coiling wave of bliss unraveled through me. Ruben had me pretty well held at my hips and the mirror supported me a little, but still, I felt as if I were crumbling, floating. I bucked for more, jerked away. It was so much and the intensity stole my breath.

My climax crested and rolled, and I opened my eyes again, concentrated on Ruben's reflection.

"Ah, yeah, squeeze me like that," he said, releasing my clit then clutching both my hips. "It's gonna make me come…ah…ah…" He tipped his face to the ceiling, closed his eyes and buried himself to the root. "Fuck, yeah…" He sucked in a deep breath. His tie settled for a second, and his chest expanded beneath his clothes.

His orgasm looked and sounded beautiful, and I knew I'd never get enough of seeing and hearing it. We were meant to be, Ruben and I. We were in perfect synchrony to weave love and time together.

He pulled out, slowly, then pushed back into me, a tremor traveling over his body and into mine.

There'd probably be bruises on my hips tomorrow but I'd wear them with pride. The way he'd enjoyed the scratch marks I'd left on his back.

"I just want to stay like this all night," he said, releasing my hip and pushing his hair from his eyes.

"Nice thought… Mmm…" I moaned as he slid almost out then pushed in again, my tender, swollen flesh hugging his cock.

He smoothed his hands over my bare buttocks. "You have such a sexy arse. Why haven't we done it like this before?"

"I'm sure there's lots of things we haven't done yet."

"Shall we make a list?" He caught my gaze in the mirror.

"That could work."

He stepped away.

I straightened and pushed my dress down to my knees, turned to him. "Do I have the just-fucked look?"

He laughed and tucked his cock away. "Yes, definitely, I wouldn't recommend going straight back downstairs."

I grabbed his tie, tugged him close. "So how about you start on that list while I go in the bathroom and freshen up?"

"I'm on it." He sealed the deal with a kiss.

* * * *

Half an hour later and looking suitably presentable, we wandered back to the reception. It had been cordoned off, so half was the noisy disco and half a quieter area with a separate bar and several soft seats. Some of the older guests were sitting there chatting, and in the corner of the room, so were Melanie and Andy.

"Shall we join them?" I asked Ruben.

"Sure, do you want a drink?"

"Just a sparkling water please."

He headed to the bar, and I joined Melanie and Andy on the brown leather L-shaped couch. They were chatting about a holiday to the Maldives they had planned.

"Hey," I said. "Can Ruben and I sit with you?"

"Absolutely," Melanie said. "We wondered where you'd gone."

A silly flush drizzled from my cheeks, onto my neck then chest. The heat of it spiked in my temples. "Oh, you know. Just for a few minutes quiet time."

Melanie laughed loudly and a little drunkenly. "So that's what it's called these days, is it? Quiet time?"

I grinned and sat. "It's been a long day, the drive up here this morning was a nightmare with the traffic. I didn't think we were going to make it at one point."

"Well you did, so that's good."

"Who drove?" Andy asked.

"Ruben."

"Oh, in his Subaru. He was telling me about that. I'll have to go check it out in the morning before we go."

"He does really like his cars," I said, looking up as he joined us with two tall glasses of water.

"Anyone else need a drink?" he asked, gesturing to Melanie's and Andy's empty wine glasses.

"Oh, white wine for me," Melanie said, holding up her glass.

"I'm good," Andy said. "Trying to make tomorrow a hangover-free day."

"Oh, hangover, shmangover," Melanie said, waving her hand in the air. "I need wine."

"I'll get it," I said, smiling at Ruben and standing. "You sit down."

"Are you sure?" He put our drinks on the table.

"Yes, absolutely." I slipped past him, giving his bum a sneaky stroke as I did so, then went to the bar.

It took a few minutes to get served, and when I did, the barman gave me the choice of pinot grigio or chardonnay. I glanced at Melanie. She was squeezing Ruben's knee and was talking animatedly, gesturing with her free hand.

"Chardonnay," I said, figuring she was pretty pissed and probably wouldn't notice or care if she switched grapes. She'd really gone for it all afternoon. It was only early evening, but she was sozzled. Who knew what she'd be like by the end of the night.

Wine in hand, I walked back over to the corner of the room. Melanie's conversation came into earshot.

"Thank goodness she's found you, Ruben. I'm so pleased to see Katie happy again, and with an extra bit of weight on her skinny bones too. You certainly are good for her."

"Hopefully," Ruben said, looking at her hand on his knee as though he wanted to remove it but wasn't sure how to do so politely.

"And as far as I'm concerned, you came along just in time," Melanie went on. "I didn't think she was ever going to get out of the hole she'd put herself in after Matt's death."

"It certainly sounds like she had a hard time," Ruben said.

"Fucking hell, yeah," Melanie slurred. "Every step has been hard, but I can't help wonder if some of the decisions she made were the right ones for her."

I paused, curious to know what Melanie thought I'd done wrong.

"Her move to Northampton?" Ruben asked, picking up his drink and poking the straw into it. The slice of lemon stuck at the base of the glass was clearly an irritation.

"Oh, no, not that, that's great, clearly, you're here. No, I'm talking about the decision to donate Matt's organs."

It was as though my blood had turned to ice. An arctic chill flooded through me. *Shit.*

"It's a very noble decision," Ruben said. "It's wonderful that people can give such an incredible gift at a time in their life when they're devastated and have lost so much."

"Yes, it is, I agree, but for Katie, well, I think it messed with her head."

Ruben turned his attention from the drink to Melanie. "What do you mean?"

"Well, she got a bit obsessed." Melanie pulled her lips down at the corners, as though trying to trap words in her mouth.

I wished she bloody well would trap them. She could then go and lock them up forever.

I took another step forward. I needed to shut her up. Now.

"Obsessed?" Ruben said, frowning. "I don't get you."

I froze. Stared at them dumbly. *I'm too late.*

"It was his heart," Melanie said, removing her hand from Ruben's knee and tapping her own chest. "She became completely obsessed with knowing who had it. It was as if finding that person would bring Matt back to her. Rubbish, I know, but grief does strange things to people. And for a while it was all she thought about—I know it was—and what's more, she told me one night that she had plans to go and find that person."

A trickle of wine slipped over my thumb, the tipping glass barely registering in my mind.

Ruben looked up.

Straight at me.

I could feel the color running from my face, my heart thumping so loudly it drowned out every other noise in the room as my pulse raged in my ears.

I righted the glass. Prayed my legs wouldn't do what they were promising and give way.

Ruben stood. He walked toward me. It was as if I were watching him move underwater or in some kind of horrible slow motion. His eyebrows hung low, and his lips parted. Disbelief and pain contorted his features.

He knew. He knew me too well. Now, instead of being a good thing, his understanding of me was going to be my undoing.

He came up close, real close, so we were chest-to-chest. He stared into my eyes.

I couldn't blink, couldn't speak.

"You tricked me," he said quietly.

"No," I whispered. "No, I didn't."

"Yes, you did." He pressed his lips together so tightly they paled and went white. His stare turned hard and cold, the softness I adored in the depths of his eyes freezing over.

"Ruben." I was trembling now. It started in my belly and was rapidly radiating to my fingers and toes and capturing everything in-between.

He shook his head. "You made me think you were in love with me when all along you were in love with what was *in* me."

"No. Please, let me explain."

He stepped back, as though I were contagious, shook his head then turned and strode from the room.

Dumbly I watched him go, his steps long and angry, his shoulders stiff and hunched.

"Are you all right?" Andy asked, appearing next to me and taking the once again spilling wine.

I turned my attention to him, then Melanie, who was looking at me from the sofa with wide eyes. "No, I'm not, Andy, not at all."

Reaching for what was left of the wine, I knocked it back in one mouthful then marched after Ruben.

I deserved a chance to explain.

Chapter Sixteen

I whacked my fist on the door of our hotel room. "Let me in, Ruben, or I'll just go and get another key from reception."

The door swung open, violently, ramming the handle against the wall. Ruben turned the instant he saw me and went to the bed.

Quickly, I followed. Halted when I saw he was throwing his shoes and wash things into his overnight bag.

"What are you doing?"

"I'm going home."

"Please no. We need to talk."

"What the fucking hell about?" He shoved his jeans into the bag then rammed the zip closed with a fast, jerking motion.

"Us." I grabbed his arm.

"Don't touch me," he said, shaking me off.

"But—"

"There's no but. Out of all the shit this crappy life has thrown at me, this is just bloody unbelievable."

"Why are you so mad?"

His face twisted. "Are you serious?"

"Yes, I'm in love with you. I thought you were with me."

"So did I until I found out you'd hunted me down."

"I didn't—" I gasped as he backed me up. But not in a super-sexy way—in a scary, he-was-mad-as-hell way.

My shoulders hit the wall. I tucked my hands beneath my chin. Felt small and vulnerable surrounded by his fury.

He slammed his hands on the either side of my head, his palms slapping against the wallpaper. He lowered his face until his nose practically touched mine.

"I just heard how you were obsessed with finding the man who had your dead husband's heart, Katie. Surprise, surprise, I happen to have received a heart. It doesn't take a genius to figure out that you came looking for me because..."

My stomach bunched. I thought I might be sick. "Because what?"

"Because I have Matt's heart." He grimaced. "And his lungs? Say it. Tell me the truth."

I nodded. "Yes. You have."

His eyes bored into mine. "Do you know how fucking sick that is?"

"Why is it?" I went to touch his chest, but he stepped away, shoving his hand into his hair and shaking his head.

"Because I've been fucking you," he said. "The man whose heart has given me life— I've been fucking his wife."

"No, it's not sick. It makes sense."

"How can you think that? You're insane."

"No I'm not. You're insane to not see it how it is."

"I'll tell you how I see it. You, Mrs. Katie Lansdale, broke—and God only knows how—every rule in the book to find me and then…then you came looking for me. I bet you couldn't believe your luck when I went and fell for your pretty face and your sweet smile and asked you out."

"No, I couldn't, because I just happen to think you're gorgeous, Ruben, and as bloody messed up as me. We were a good match. We *are* a good match."

"Messed up? Speak for yourself. I'm nowhere near as loopy as you are." He twirled his finger by his ear.

"You have no idea what I went through—"

"And you have no idea what I went through. Living a half-life, praying for a miracle and then clawing my way back to health. That wasn't exactly a picnic, you know, and then, just as I feel like I have something to look forward to—you—it's pulled from under me."

"Why is it? You still have me."

"But I don't want you. Don't you see?" He shook his head.

I thought I saw tears in his eyes, but he turned away, reached for his car keys.

"No, I don't see. Why don't you want me?"

"Because I'm not who you think I am, Katie. Not who you think you're in love with, and I can't live with someone who doesn't love me for me." He rubbed at his eyes harshly. "I'm not Matt. I might have his heart, his lungs, but I'm not him. He simply gave me something to pump blood and oxygen around my body."

"No, no, that's not right." I raised my voice, anger replacing the panic of him leaving. "*I* gave you that heart." I stabbed my chest with my finger. "It was *me* that made the decision. I was his next of kin. I held my husband's hand then picked up a pen and signed that heart over to you. You're alive, Ruben, because I made it that way. Without me, you'd be as dead as Matt is."

He clenched his jaw, picked up his bag and tilted his chin. "Goodbye, Katie."

Goodbye! "Don't go. We can talk about this. We can work it out, I know we can."

"This." He flicked his car keys between us. "Is a relationship based on a lie. So many times you could have told me the truth but you didn't, and I have to ask myself why that is."

I stilled. "What do you mean?"

He was silent for a long moment, and I thought he might not explain himself, then, "You look at me and you see him, don't you?"

"No, not at all. Ruben, I see *you*." I pressed my shaking fingertips to my lips. "And you know about Matt now, so let's work it out."

"No. It's too late. Your lie… It went on for too long." He swept past me and pulled the door open. "Please don't ever try and find me again. Once was enough." He released the handle and let the door slam behind him.

I stared at the swaying Do Not Disturb sign.

It was then my legs gave up. I dropped to the bed, anger and despair bursting molten hot tears from my eyes and ransacking my chest in heaving sobs.

This was never meant to happen. I'd been wrong to find him in the first place and wrong to go and see him. But I'd been dating Ruben. I'd fallen for him. He got me, made me feel better. How could he think that I didn't love him for him? He'd become my entire world. Thank goodness he had Matt's heart. Thank goodness I'd made the decision that Melanie had thought so wrong, because if I hadn't, Ruben wouldn't be on this earth for me to love.

I buried my face in the cover, uncaring of the wet mess I was making. Banging my legs in frustration, I then thumped a pillow.

Once again it struck me how quickly life could change. Only an hour ago I had been making plans to move in with a man I'd fallen in love with, a man I wanted to hitch my wagon to and ride off into the sunset with, and now…now I was alone, again.

I sucked in a breath, sat and pushed my hair from my face, anger suddenly my overwhelming emotion.

How dare he? How dare he just presume that I thought of him as Matt? After everything we'd done? Our relationship had been intense, growing in passion both emotionally and physically. Did he really think I could fake that, or — and this was a worse thought — did he think I had twisted ideas that I was giving Matt a blow job, fucking Matt somehow when I was with him?

Really? Did he think I was *that* loopy?

I stood, wiped my nose on the back of my hand then reached for my purse. I pulled my wedding ring from the side pocket and held it to the light by the mirror.

I'd taken it off because new Katie had arrived. New Katie was moving forward, falling in love, making new friends — planning a future that held endless possibilities. It had been scary to shake my grief, I realized that now. Grief had been a heavy blanket I'd worn like a shield. It could keep people out.

But I'd let Ruben in, welcomed him with open arms. Let him see my wounds and scars. Not as visible as his, but still as deep.

"Don't ever try and find me again," I said to the ring. "How can the man I love be alive and me not be with him?" I shook my head at this novel concept, this whole new, imaginative way to have my world torn in two, my heart broken.

Through the center of the ring I saw the mirror. I could just make out two handprints—mine, my sweaty palms had left a smudge. I could hear our gasps and moans, the power of my orgasm. Hell, my pussy still felt inflamed.

Suddenly it was as if the walls were looming down on me, oppressive and suffocating.

I had to get out of there.

I tucked the ring into my purse, kicked off my stilettoes then rammed my feet into flats.

Slipping into the corridor, I turned right toward reception. I thought I'd made it without seeing any wedding guests—goodness only knew what a mess I looked—but then Andy and Melanie came around the corner. He was supporting her. She walked with her head on his shoulder and her eyes closed.

"Shit, Katie, are you all right?" Andy asked me again, no doubt taking in my odd shoe choice with my dress and my wild hair and makeup.

"No, Andy, I'm not." I kept on walking. I wasn't in a chatty mood.

"Where are you going?" he asked. "Katie?"

"To see Matt," I shouted as I marched through the foyer and out into the cool night.

A taxi sat in the hotel car park, and I climbed in the back seat and agitatedly buckled up.

"Where to, love?" the driver asked, switching the radio down.

"Hill Rise Crem, please."

He turned and studied me over the rim of his glasses. "You're pulling my leg, right?"

"Do I look like I'm in a joking mood?" I shooed my hand at the road. "Step on it."

"Okay, but I think they're all tucked up for the night." He started the engine then pulled away. "The party here is much livelier by the sounds of it."

I tutted and set my stare out of the window.

The orange glow of streetlamps flickered past—even though it wasn't completely dark yet they'd come on.

As we drew to a stop at the entrance of Hill Rise, the sky was slashed with violent orange and reds on the western horizon. The spiked treetops and the chimney of the crematorium were silhouetted against the fiery backdrop like cardboard cutouts.

"You want me to wait, love? It'll be pitch dark up there soon."

I handed him a twenty. "No, but will you come back in an hour?"

"Can't guarantee it will be on the dot, but I'll swing back at some point before the end of my shift at eleven and if you're here, I'll take you home."

"Thanks."

I climbed out onto the pebbled path. The taxi pulled away, its wheels rudely loud in the silent cemetery. When the lights had gone from view, I started my slow walk to Matt's grave.

I wasn't completely sure why I was here. It was more not knowing where else to be than heading to the cemetery for a reason. I didn't belong anywhere anymore—and not with anyone. That flailing feeling was back. Falling without a parachute. Someone had taken the safety net from under my tightrope and I was crashing down.

Stomping up the hill—the earth hard and solid beneath my feet—I reached the large new angel with her spread wings. I paused. On the stone beneath her a flickering candle was still burning. Someone had been to that grave recently. I wondered if it were a child's.

I turned and saw the small set of headstones I was heading for. A coolish breeze touched my cheeks, pulling more straggling locks of hair from my once neat style.

As if hair was of any concern to me.

I was a woman who had nothing left. Not even the emotional tools to rebuild from here. I was empty. I'd run out of everything.

"No," I said, making a fist. "Be strong, Katie."

But could I? I'd been as strong as I could be. I'd smiled, I'd eaten, I'd balanced on the tightrope. What if I really was all used up? What if my energy just didn't equal my will to carry on?

I reached Matt's grave.

An owl hooted in a nearby tree.

"Matt," I whispered. I knew he wasn't really there, but still, I liked his name on my tongue. "Matt, I've messed up." As I spoke, tears sprang forth again. In a gush this time, not even individual drips, just streams and rivers pouring down my face.

I dropped to my knees, fell forward, forehead on the ground above his buried urn. I'd run out of strength. It was official. My body was tired, exhausted, but more than that, my emotions were wrung out. Battered and bruised, I didn't have the energy to sift through the pain. It was just one big, nasty lump of agony, black and sticky and cancerous. It made me bleed inside. It blurred my vision and ate away at any tiny fragment of hope I had left.

I was hopeless.

I became aware of a gentle pressure on my right shoulder.

"Shit!" I sprang forward, grabbed Matt's headstone and turned. Fight or flight kicked in. I should never have come here at night.

"I'm sorry. I didn't mean to scare you." Ruben held up his hands, as if in surrender.

I stared at him, thankful it wasn't a weirdo or a ghost but wanting to slap him for the freaky fright. "Sneaking up on someone at night in a cemetery," I panted through my lingering sobs. "That's a damn sure way to scare someone." I stayed crouched over, wondering if my heart would survive the scare.

"I'm sorry," he said again, dropping his hands to his sides and shaking his head.

"What are you doing here?" My legs were watery. I fought to stay upright. "How did you know where I was?"

"I went back to talk to you and saw Andy staggering along with a very drunk Melanie." He stared at me, and through the dim light and I could tell he was frowning. "He said you'd gone to see Matt. I guessed that meant here. Melanie opened her eyes long enough to tell me the name of the cemetery."

"But? It's…" I motioned my arm around the sea of stones. "Huge."

"I saw your silhouette, when you stopped by the angel over there."

I stared at the tall, dark statue, her wingtips pointing heavenward, her head bowed in prayer.

"But I thought you never wanted to see me again. Why would you follow me?" I couldn't understand what he was doing here, after what he'd said back at the hotel.

"Katie." He touched his forehead, rubbed his temple. "I've got to figure this out. It's kind of a shock, you know." He paused.

I didn't fill the silence.

"Just tell me what the bloody hell was going through your mind," he said.

"What do you mean?"

"When you thought it was okay to get involved with the man who had your dead husband's heart beating in his chest." He pressed his hand over his sternum. "And air in his lungs."

I moved behind Matt's stone, gripped the top of it and looked warily at Ruben. He didn't seem mad anymore, just confused. But still, I knew he could hurt me—not physically, but with words. Any type of shield was welcome. I had no defenses left.

"I didn't think anything."

"Of course you did."

"No, not once I got to know you. It was just you."

"Okay." He nodded slowly. "And at what point was that? The once-you-got-to-know-me bit?"

As another hoot rang out, I glanced in the direction of the owl. "I suppose it was when we went to the champagne bar."

He tugged on his bottom lip with his finger. "That's good."

"It is?"

"Yes." He paused. "So in the park, when we first met…?"

I shrugged, stiffly.

"Katie?"

"I spoke to the transplant coordinator. She said that the recipient may choose to get in touch with me to express gratitude at some point, but it was no guarantee, and they wouldn't give me any information about you other than your gender, age and that the initial operation had gone well." I paused, swallowed. "I thought about writing to you. She said I could do that, but it wasn't what I wanted. I wanted to see you. So at the museum, yes, I was curious. I was there to catch a glimpse of the recipient. I'll admit that."

He shook his head. "The *recipient*? Is that how you see me?"

"Back then, yes. I didn't know you. But that was all I wanted to do, see you, from a distance. By then I had your name and knew you worked at the museum—no other details." I brushed the dusty grit off the top of Matt's stone, sweeping it left and right down its arced shape. It was so quiet I could hear the grains rubbing on the marble. "I didn't plan on talking to you. I just…" It all seemed so long ago now. The intensity of my time with Ruben had faded it into the past.

"Go on."

"It's hard to explain," I said.

"Try, Katie. For God's sake try, will you?" There was anguish in his tone.

I looked up at him. He was slumped, apparently as tired and beaten as me.

"I just needed to know what you looked like," I said. "I couldn't sleep. When I did, I dreamt of Matt. I just felt that being able to picture where his heart was would help. It was a thought that grew bigger and bigger until it couldn't be ignored, couldn't be contained. It had given me some focus when I was stumbling around blindly."

"So you had someone find me. How the hell did you manage that?"

"Does it matter?"

He was quiet, then, "I suppose not." He shrugged. "You did, and that's the point."

"Yes, but honestly, I just needed to know where the heart was that had loved me so much."

Ruben touched his chest and rubbed his palm up to his throat.

"And then that damn Blitz room and the crazy peacock threw us together, and it was you who asked me to the café. It was you who asked me out, remember? I didn't pursue you at all. You gave me your number."

"Of course I remember. I was there."

I stepped around the gravestone, gathered my last tiny vestige of strength and stood tall. "I'll admit I was fascinated at the thought of Matt's heart inside you, a tiny bit of him that was still living. It's a strange concept, but that didn't make you him, Ruben. You're you, a speed junkie, Formula One nut, and all round funny but sensitive bloke." I paused. "I never once was with you and pretended I was with Matt. Not once."

"You didn't?"

"No, no of course not. I promise you that." I shook my head. "Matt's dead." I pointed at the ground. I'd never get used to saying those words, but I couldn't change the truth.

Ruben took a step closer, his expression a mixture of pain and confusion. He held out one hand. A wave of fear coursed through me. I couldn't take rejection again. If I let Ruben get close, he might push me away. Might say what a loopy cow I was and order me never to go near him again. Hell, he could get me in a whole pile of trouble for hunting him down. There were rules and laws and ethical issues that should have stopped me.

I turned, faced the twilight sky.

"Katie—"

"Ruben, no. I've been running low on emotional strength for years, but right now I'm on empty. Please, if you have to leave, just leave."

"I don't want to leave. I want to understand this."

"I've explained all that I can. It's quite simple really. We met, fell in love and you happen to have had an organ transplant from someone I also loved."

"But don't you see that stirs up so many questions?" He rested his hands on my shoulders, brushed my neck with his thumbs.

I resisted the urge to fall back against him. He was way too tempting. Everything about him enticed me. But what if he stepped away? How would I get up again?

I stared into the distance, consciously pulling and pushing my breaths in and out of my lungs. "Questions?" I asked eventually.

"Yes," he said softly, "if this heart that's in me loved you before, then is that why I love you so much now that I can't even think straight when I'm not with you?"

"Don't say it." I turned, a frantic spin that knocked me into him. "Don't say you love me if you're not going to do anything with those words." A lump caught in my throat. "That's just cruel, Ruben, and I can't take any more pain."

"Damn it, I don't want to cause you pain, but you've made this so complicated." He gripped the top of my arms. "How can I ever know if you truly love me or if what I'm feeling for you is real?"

"He just brought us together," I said, reading the inscription, *Matthew Lincoln Lansdale* on the stone. "Matt just brought us together. That's how I look at it. He didn't want me to be alone. You said that yourself.

This is his way—or fate's way—of making sure we both have what we need. Each other."

Ruben was quiet, the line between his eyebrows deep as my words settled. "Perhaps I can look at it like that," he said. "That he brought us together, like this was mapped out in the stars or something."

A nugget of hope, when I thought I had none, sprang to life. "And if you can?"

"And if I can…"

I felt as if I were spinning, the disco lights from earlier bouncing around me. I had to catch them, those lights. They were my future—all I had left.

He cupped my face in his palms. The softness was back in his eyes.

Could he really figure out a new way to understand this? Make peace with what had happened and move on, even after he'd been so angry with me? So confused.

"And if I can, and if you'll have me," he said, his lips a whisper from mine, "then I want to be with you for all of time."

"Ruben, I—"

"It's messed up and weird as hell, but I can't imagine living without you, Katie, not now."

He kissed me as a sob bubbled up from my chest. I clung to him. In a sudden rush, happiness blustered beneath me, whisking me up to my tightrope. I could balance up there again, happily, with Ruben at my side. This was a good place to be.

"I'm sorry," he said, pulling back. "For being so mad. Really sorry."

"It was a shock for you." I grasped his arms, felt his familiar shape beneath his jacket and breathed in his comforting scent. "And I'm sorry too, for not telling you."

"I know you are," he said. "And it *was* a shock. It still is, but I'll get used to it. You have."

"Yes, for me it's helped everything make sense."

He stroked his thumbs over my cheeks. I hadn't realized they were so wet with tears. "It just took me a little while," he whispered, "to realize that you're an angel, Katie, an angel who has been hiding her wings."

Chapter Seventeen

I stared up at him. The shadows of the night sliced across his features, and his eyes sparkled with emotion. His was the face that I dreamed of now, the one I wanted to see at the end of the day, the one that held my future.

"Ruben," I managed, my throat tight. "I think angel may be stretching it a bit."

"No." He shook his head and frowned slightly. "You're right. I have you to thank that I'm not six feet under. You made that brave decision when your world was in tatters."

I shook my head. Shrugged. "It just felt right when everything else felt so wrong."

"Thank goodness it felt right. But don't you see? To give something so precious to a stranger... That makes you a very special person."

"I—"

He interrupted me again, this time with a kiss.

I melted against him. Our lips were a little salty with my tears, and my cheeks, despite the cool, were hot.

"I knew you were special from the first time I saw you," he murmured, slipping his hands around my body and spanning his palms on my back. "Through the gloom and the explosions of the Blitz room, and then outside when you were flapping your bag at the peacock." A slight smile tugged his mouth. "I knew then. I was drawn to you. It was…"

"What?" I asked when he seemed to be struggling to find the words. "What was it?"

"You looked so sad," he said, frowning. "And so delicate, like a beautiful china doll that needed taking care of."

"I was sad." I nodded and smoothed the lapel of his jacket. "And confused, and scared of the future. I didn't realize it at the time, but looking back I wasn't thinking straight. I shouldn't have sought you out. That was wrong of me."

"But thank goodness you did."

I reached up and cupped his cheek. The faint prickle of evening stubble tickled my skin. To hear him say that was like a big eraser rubbing away the angry words he'd spoken earlier.

"I've never thought of myself as delicate," I said, "but…"

"But you were. How could you not be? That night at the champagne bar, all I wanted to do was wrap my arms around you and protect you from the big bad world—make sure nothing ever hurt you again." He pulled me a little closer.

A shiver wound through me. It was getting colder by the minute.

He ran his hands up and down my back, creating a little friction to warm my flesh. "And that's still what I want to do. Make sure nothing or no one ever hurts you again."

"But you could hurt me," I said, my throat tightening with emotion as I remembered the agony of only an hour ago when he'd slammed out of the hotel room and told me never to seek him out. Once again my life had been turned on its head, my innards twisted then dropped into a heavy pit of despair. Ruben had the ability to hurt me more than anyone else on the planet, simply by not being there, not wanting me.

"I'm so sorry, so really bloody sorry," he said. "I shouldn't have let my temper flow like that. It's not who I am. I don't blow my top, I—"

"Shh." I rubbed my hand over his face and pressed my index finger to his lips. "Shh, it was extenuating circumstances. I understand. You were upset." I moved my finger.

"I'm sorry," he said again. "For shouting, for backing you up. I didn't mean to frighten you, or—"

"You didn't." He had, but I could keep that to myself. "I know you, Ruben. I know you'd never physically hurt me, but…"

"But what?"

"But please…don't…"

"Katie?" He brushed his lips over mine. "What?"

"Just don't leave me. It would destroy me. I don't think I could climb out of hell again."

"I won't leave you. I promise. I love you. I love you so damn much it hurts. And if I didn't have you… If you didn't want me, then I don't know how I would go on."

I blinked rapidly, trying and failing to stave off a fresh batch of tears.

He kissed both my cheeks, his touch warm and soft. "Looks like we're well and truly stuck with each other, then," he whispered, his breath warm.

"Yes. It does." A slightly out of control giggle, mixed with a sob burst up from my chest. It was as though my feelings, the whole spectrum of them, were pinging around inside me, ricocheting around my body and exploding like tiny fireworks.

He pulled me closer, tucking my head beneath his chin.

"We should get out of here," he said. "You're cold. That dress is hardly designed for outdoors at night."

I nodded and suppressed another shiver. I was cold, but I also didn't want to untwine myself from Ruben. It didn't matter what else was going on. If I was in his arms, it would all be okay.

He dropped a kiss to my head. "Come on, let's go back to the hotel."

I nodded as he slipped his jacket off and wrapped it around my shoulders. It had absorbed his body heat, which I welcomed, as it spread over my shoulders and arms. I liked the weight of the jacket too. It was real and embraced me the way Ruben's arms did.

Matt's gravestone stood sentry-like next to us, the shiny surface dull without the daylight bouncing off it. I hadn't seen it at night before and it harnessed my attention.

Ruben rubbed his hand over my shoulders and hugged me against his side. "Are you ready to go?" He paused, studying my face. "We can stay longer if you want to."

I shook my head. "No, I'm ready to go. I don't know why I came here really. I've never been one for using a stone and a patch of earth as a symbol of my loss. It's so much bigger than that when someone dies. Loss is there at breakfast, lunch, when you go to bed, when you get up. It's there at Christmas and birthdays, when something funny happens and you want to share it." I swallowed and looked up at Ruben. "For so long, my grief ate me up. It was like being chewed up over and over then spat out at the end of each day." I huffed, frustrated by my way of explaining it. "It was exhausting. So damn tiring." I sighed. "But now, with you, lately, I haven't been so tired. I've wanted to eat, wanted to sleep, wanted to get up in the morning and think of the future."

"Our future?" His expression was serious.

"Yes. Our future." Another shiver attacked my spine. My teeth clattered a little. "We should go."

Ruben frowned and rubbed my shoulder. "We can come back here anytime. It's not far from Northampton. I'll drive you."

"No, it's okay." I paused and looked at the dark earth where I'd knelt earlier. "I don't need to be here, not like his parents do. For them it's a way to show their respect and gives them a focus. Something to still do for their son."

Ruben was quiet. It was as if he knew I was working through my thoughts.

"For me," I said, "I'll show my respect for Matt by giving happiness another go. Honoring his memory by not dying alongside him."

"I will make you happy," Ruben said, determination in his tone. "I'll spend the rest of my life making you happy. That is how I'll repay my gratitude to you and Matt for what I have now. I'll adore you, protect you, do anything for you, the way Matt did—still would if it hadn't been for the accident. That's what I'll do. Don't ever doubt it, Katie."

I tore my attention from the ground. Life was such a precious and fragile thing, the same as happiness was. It made sense that the two should go hand in hand,

and that both were worth fighting for. "And I hope I can make you happy too."

"You already have." He tightened his grip on me and stepped forward. "You already have, more than you'll ever know."

I fell into pace at his side, gripping the front of his jacket at my chest to keep precious heat in. My feet were damp now, the night dew tapping over the rim of the shoes. I could see a little mist puffing from my mouth as I walked.

Silently we navigated through the rows of stones. I kept my attention on the angel in the distance. She was my beacon in the darkness and her wings seemed to glow, as though they'd absorbed the daylight that had previously streamed down on them.

As we drew closer, I stared up at her serene face. Her eyes were downcast, her mouth neither smiling nor sad. She was neutral. For a while I'd thought that was the best I could hope for again, to just not be in agony. But I'd been lucky enough to find a way to smile. A map that showed me where happiness and contentment lived. A good and kind man to hold my hand and walk the journey with me.

I moved a little closer to Ruben, our hips bumping slightly as we walked past the angel. The candle at her feet had gone out now. Stolen by the night.

"I'm just down there," Ruben said, nodding in the direction of the car park.

"Okay." I could see his Subaru. It was the only vehicle at the crem.

We weaved around a couple of larger, tomb-like graves then onto a gravel path. Soon we were at Ruben's car, and he took his keys from his trouser pocket. He pointed them at the car and it beeped and flashed to life.

"In you get," he said, opening the passenger door.

I climbed in and pulled on my seatbelt.

Ruben dropped into the driver side, the engine rumbled and he flicked the heating to full blast. "Soon have you warm," he said, turning on the lights.

They lit up the darkness, the long beam sliding over the grass and reaching up the hill.

"I'm not that cold," I said. "I'm okay."

"You sure?"

"Yes, really. Much better than when I arrived here."

"Me too." He reached across and pressed a kiss to my cheek. "Me too."

* * * *

I soon warmed up on the drive back to the hotel and the footwell heater soothed my cold toes.

"Did you say Melanie was going to bed?" I asked as we turned at the brilliantly lit hotel sign.

"Yes, she was past it," Ruben said. "Peaked too early."

"Mmm." I knew I should be cross with her, furious in fact for revealing my secret. But I didn't have the energy. And well, perhaps it was for the best that the truth had been exposed. I hadn't realized it, but like grief, keeping something from someone special was also a weight to be borne and carried around each day. I felt lighter for it being out in the open, for not having to wonder anymore what Ruben would think if he knew. It was there on the table for him to see.

Maybe one day I'd even thank her.

Maybe.

Ruben pulled to a stop and turned off the engine. The silence was suddenly deafening. I could hear my pulse in my ears. My thoughts seemed to tumble and rattle around my skull.

I turned to him. He was staring at me.

"What?" I whispered.

"I just need to be with you," he said.

"You are."

"No." He shook his head. "Naked, as close as we can be. I just need...you."

My thoughts calmed, as did the raging noise in my ears. It was simple really. So simple. We just needed each other. We just needed to be together. "You have me."

"Not quite where I want you," he said. His mouth stretched into the bad-boy smile I adored, the one that always appeared when he was thinking dirty thoughts.

"Well, I think you should rectify that situation immediately," I said.

"Yes, you're absolutely right."

He pulled the keys from the ignition and stepped out of the car. He walked to my side and opened the door. He looked so tall and determined standing there, his energy and attention all focused on me.

A thrill shot through my body. He was right. We did just need to get naked and as close as two people could physically be.

Still with his jacket around my shoulders, I allowed him to steer me into the hotel. The lights were bright and the beat of the disco thudded over the hard floor and into the vaulted glass ceiling. With each step, I felt both a calmness and a longing weave through me — a curious mixture of emotions that swirled together.

As we walked past the door to the disco, the sound of the music increased. It was some sixties track that always got played at parties and everyone was singing along and waving their hands in the air. I spotted the bride, dancing wildly with her new husband. The demureness of earlier long gone as she held her dress around her knees and kicked off her heels. Her hair had tumbled down around her face and her cheeks glowed pink.

Ruben paused. "Do you want to go in?"

"No." I quickly shook my head. "I only want to be with you. I feel…exhausted."

"I'm not surprised." He took my hand and we carried on down the winding corridor before we eventually came to a halt at our room.

I stared at the door, thought of him slamming out of it earlier then forced away the image. I didn't want to remember that—now we were going to make another new memory, a happy one. I didn't have room for bad ones to haunt me.

Ruben opened the door, and I stepped inside. I hung his jacket on a hook and kicked off my shoes. A few strands of grass had attached themselves to my foot.

"I might take a shower," I said, stooping to pick the blades off.

He glanced at the bed, then at me.

"Want to join me?" I asked, straightening.

"Yes." A small muscle flexed then unflexed in his cheek as he started to undo the buttons on his shirt.

I smiled and went into the bathroom. The walls were covered in large glossy cream tiles. The suite was white and the taps and showerhead chrome. It had a wide mirror over the sink with small lights around it and a separate bath on squat legs.

But it was a shower that I wanted. That would be quicker than a bath, which in turn meant I'd be in bed, with Ruben, all the sooner.

I flicked on the faucet then glanced in the mirror.

I tutted. Stuck in my fringe was a tuft of dry grass and on my forehead a smudge of earth. The ground had been dry but I guessed my tears had muddied it, leaving a mark on my head. I pulled away a lock of hair that had glued itself to the smear. I'd have to wash it.

Ruben's reflection appeared next to mine. His chest was bare, and I guessed, so was his lower half.

"I look a mess," I said.

"You look beautiful. You always do."

"That's kind but…" I scowled at my flushed cheeks and the redness on my puffy eyelids.

"There's no but about it. You, Katie, are beautiful. To me there has never been anyone more beautiful."

I smiled at that.

He returned the grin and reached for the zipper on my dress. Slowly he pulled it down.

The mirror was starting to mist up but I could study his expression as he looked at my back.

The dress loosened and he hooked his fingers beneath the shoulder straps then eased them down my arms. The dress slithered over my body and landed in a crumpled heap around my feet.

He kissed my shoulder and a pleasant shiver ran through me, spiking my nipples and making goosebumps rise around my nape.

I pushed at my knickers, sent them down my legs then kicked them aside.

"Come on," he said, taking my hand in his. With the other he tested the temperature of the water. "Let's wash all this upset away."

"Yes." I allowed him to tug me into the large, glass shower cubicle. The water was deliciously hot and had a strong force.

Instantly Ruben's hair soaked through and flattened to his head. He smiled at me as the water ran over his face, sliding in rivulets from his chin. It made his chest hair stick to his skin, the long scar becoming wet and shiny.

I moved closer to him, touched the top of his scar and slid my finger, gently, slowly, down the mark.

He stilled and watched my movements. It wasn't that I hadn't touched it before. I had. It was just now he knew the truth I'd been keeping from him.

I leaned forward and kissed it, the water running over my head and face as my lips connected.

I sensed him holding his breath. I looked up at him. "I love you, every piece of you."

He exhaled, his expression softened. "I know."

I smiled and straightened, my hair fell over my eyes and I pushed at it.

"Turn around," he said, touching my shoulder.

I did as he'd asked, stared at the faucet that had a chrome lever with arrows indicating hot and cold.

His hands were in my hair. I could smell something sweet and soapy — shampoo — as he set about creating a lather.

I shut my eyes and relaxed into his caring touch.

His big fingers circled over my scalp, rubbed to the ends of my hair and massaged over my head.

I sighed and leaned back against him.

His solid, steady body supported me and he carried on filling my hair with suds. My emotions felt bruised, my body so tired. What he was doing was perfect.

How did he just know what I needed?

Earlier, fast and passion-fueled had suited us. Now was all about the slow and indulgent.

He moved me beneath the water and let it soak through my hair. The suds washed down my body as he rubbed them free. His erection jutted against the small of my back, his wiry body hair tickling my skin.

Eventually he turned me to face him.

I opened my eyes and stared into his.

My heart rate picked up. I saw such love in his face. This was all so right. It was all going to stay all right.

"I think you're done," he said, smiling. "You'd gathered quite a bit of mud on your head and collected some grass in your hair."

"I didn't realize." I pushed it back from my brow. "Thank you."

"It's my pleasure." He bit on his bottom lip and grinned. "Come on—time to get out of here." He stepped from the cubicle, wrapped a towel around his waist then held one wide for me.

I walked into it, happy to have his arms lock around me as the soft material caressed my skin.

His chin was against my temple and his breaths breezed over me.

I studied our blurred reflections in the steamy mirror. We looked good together. There was no denying that. Two lost souls who'd finally found each other and shaken the shackles of deception, the ball and chain of grief and the prison sentence of illness.

Epilogue

Six Months Later

I sank my feet into the warm Caribbean sand and let it tumble over my toes. The sea breeze lifted my veil, tugging where the comb fastened it to my hair at the crown of my head. Ruben took both my hands in his and smiled down at me.

He looked healthy and gorgeous with his new tan, wearing a white linen shirt matched with cream chinos. I could hardly believe he was going to be my husband in just a few minutes. Those soft, dreamy eyes of his that understood me so well, that had captured my soul, were going to be mine to gaze into for all of time.

I glanced at my parents and Trevor and Veronica — our only guests — standing on the beach a few feet away. The ladies were in floral dresses — my mother's a wash of plum-purples and bruised-berries, Veronica's a dolly mixture of pinks, oranges and violets. They both had feathered fascinators in their hair, similar, because they'd shopped together the week before—two giggling ladies excited about their trip to Barbados and a wedding. The men wore short-sleeved shirts and ties, the colors matching their respective spouse with devastating accuracy, their hair freshly trimmed and their cheeks and chins devoid of any holiday stubble.

"Katie?" Ruben asked, harnessing my attention once more.

I squeezed his hands. Smiled. It was perfect. When Ruben had proposed to me three months ago, he'd said he wanted me to make new wedding day memories and we could do it where and however I wanted.

Saying our vows on a beach seemed the perfect way to bless our union. Instead of roses I had orchids, instead of a churchyard, our photographs would have the ocean as the backdrop. This was my wedding to Ruben. It went into a different folder from my wedding to Matt. Not better, not worse, just different.

And I loved Ruben every bit as much as I'd loved Matt. My heart was full of it, swollen with it. Every cell in my body was tuned into being with him. My good fortune to find the grand but humble emotion of love again was not lost on me—not one bit. I would be eternally grateful.

"Are you ready?" the officiator asked.

"Yes," I said, nodding. "Absolutely."

The short ceremony began. I only stumbled a little, on 'until death do us part' but Ruben had pre-empted this and smoothed his thumbs over the inside of my wrists as the words were spoken, letting me know he was there, that he understood this bit was hard. Not just because I'd lost Matt but because he'd always have to take that extra bit of care of himself too. We couldn't take anything for granted, that wasn't how it was for us.

Ruben slipped a white-gold ring onto my finger, saying solemnly what it meant. My balance quavered, but in a good way—in a way that made me want to throw my arms around him and tell him how happy his words made me. That kind of wobble I could live with. It was light and feathery, made me want to fly.

I slid a thicker, matching band onto his finger, loving the symbolism and the fact it made him mine, that it tied us together. Husband and wife.

As a wave burst and its skittering, frothy edge nearly reached us, Ruben was told to kiss his bride. He gathered me close, fitting my body into his and took possession of my mouth. I melted against him. Nothing I could say could express my happiness—actions the only thing that could come anywhere near to doing justice to the enormous bouncing ball of joy.

Another sweep of breeze tickled over us, pressing my long white silky dress to my legs and curling my veil around our faces. I pushed it back, laughing, and saw exhilaration and love in Ruben's eyes as he released me.

I turned to our parents.

There was a rush of congratulations and kisses, hugs and slaps on the back. Everyone was smiling, both mothers had moist eyes and they each held damp tissues.

"I'm so happy for you," Veronica said, squeezing me close. "You and Ruben couldn't be more perfect for one another."

"I agree," I said, embracing her.

"You gave him a future we never thought he'd have. For that I'm so indebted, Katie."

I pulled back and studied her face. Ruben and I hadn't told anyone, not a soul, that he had Matt's heart. Melanie had certainly never guessed, and I hadn't brought up the subject with her on the few occasions we'd got together. But had Ruben told his mother in a quiet moment? Shared the details of what I'd done?

"Maybe one day even a future with children," she said, cupping my cheek.

I looked into her eyes, trying to see if there was some other knowledge there. I couldn't be sure.

She smiled. "You'll have beautiful babies, Katie. You really are the prettiest bride I've ever seen." She hugged me again. "Simply breathtaking."

If she did know anything, I wasn't about to question it — not today, and probably not ever. My history had found a place to settle, a place where it could wait until the days I chose to bring it out and visit it. Finally, the past had moved from my present back to where it belonged.

"Come on," Ruben said, reaching for my hand. "Time for the wedding feast."

I laughed, scooped up the hem of my dress and walked behind him, sinking my bare feet into the sand and puffing up little grainy clouds behind me. "You've been looking forward to this bit, haven't you?"

"You know I have, the menu looks delicious." He released my hand, pulled me close and pressed his mouth to my ear. "Plus I have to keep my strength up for my wedding night. I reckon I'll be using up quite a bit of energy."

* * * *

We dined on flying fish and cou cou, roast pork with diamond crackling, chicken stuffed with spiced rice and yams, sweet potato and pumpkin—more food than we needed and all vibrant, fresh, delicious, served to us by discreet, courteous staff in white suits.

We were seated within a thatched cabana, still close to the waves, the Caribbean winds keeping us from overheating and the cocktails holding our thirst at bay. I couldn't stop touching Ruben—even when eating I still needed that physical contact.

It seemed he did, too, and every few minutes he stroked my cheek, my shoulder or my thigh beneath the table. Whenever I looked at him, he was looking at me.

Our parents had hit it off from the first time they'd met, the men sharing a common interest in golf, and our mothers, shopping. Mine had been floored by my grief and hadn't known how to help me. But then who could? I'd folded into my shroud of misery and it had taken Ruben coming under with me to persuade me to stop wearing it.

My parents—seeing me no longer a ghost of myself, but Katie, their daughter who laughed and joked—had an extra lining to their happiness today. I knew they did. They'd told me so. Seeing me happy and back in the land of the living was a dream come true for them.

Eventually the sun started to set. The chocolate icebox pudding and lemon meringues we'd indulged in had been cleared away, and shadows from the nearby palm trees sent thin fluttering fingers of light elongating over the table.

"Right," Trevor said, plucking four strips of paper from his wallet. "I think it's time to leave these lovebirds to it and go and see the limbo dancing."

"What?" I said with a laugh. "Limbo dancing?"

"Yes," he said. "Four tickets for Fire Limbo Extraordinaire." He read the wording on the tickets. "Prepare to be dazzled, stunned and heated up to boiling point by men and women who can move to the groove and get down to the ground."

My mother giggled and nudged Veronica. "Sounds fun. What do you think?"

"Sounds like a cultural experience." Veronica nodded, her eyes wide and looking a little unsure.

I caught my dad's gaze and grinned. His cheeks had flushed with the cocktails, and he looked more content than I'd seen him in a long time.

"Are you sure you two aren't coming?" he asked. "We could get extra tickets."

"Oh, no," Ruben said quickly. "We have a romantic stroll along the beach planned for our first evening as husband and wife."

"That sounds lovely," my mother said, placing her napkin on the table and standing. "And you couldn't have chosen a nicer spot to enjoy a walk."

"It is stunning, isn't it," I said, looking at the near deserted beach that stretched into the distance.

Hues of gold and amber created a magical glow, and the ocean was turning deep blackcurrant. The sand was lined with a scramble of foliage—ferns, palms and huge cerise flowers that I didn't know the name of. The outline of a tumbling mountain, also a mass of greenery, paraded into the sea as though guarding our hotel resort.

After more hugs, plans to meet for lunch the next day in the hotel's rooftop café, and Trevor's excited rush to head off to see the limbo dancing, Ruben and I walked to the water's edge.

He rested his hand on my shoulder, and I slipped my arm around his waist. I lifted my dress just high enough so the salty water didn't catch the hem.

"This has been wonderful," he said, pressing a kiss to the top of my head. "Everything I hoped it would be when we were planning it."

"I agree. What a place. Do you think our parents enjoyed it?"

"I don't think you need to ask. I haven't seen my mother smile so much for years. She's completely in love with you."

"Is she?" I asked.

"Yes, she told me a while ago how perfect you are for me. That she couldn't imagine me with anyone else."

"That's nice." I paused. "Did you…?" *I should ask…ask if he took that conversation elsewhere.*

"Did I what?"

But I couldn't. What would I do with the answer? There was no point in digging up something that would be of no value. "Did your dad have fun too?"

"Of course. If Mum's happy, he's happy." He pointed into the distance. "Do you really want to do this walk? It's a long way and our villa is only there."

I glanced to the right. Our secluded straw-roofed luxury hut could be made out through several twisted trees and a couple of unruly bushes. A winding path of driftwood planks, lit with the occasional solar light, led the way to the verandah.

"Not if you don't want to," I said.

"It's not that I don't want to." He stooped and swung me into his arms in a sudden burst of energy. "I'm just keen to consummate our marriage."

"Ruben." I laughed and linked my hands behind his neck. "What are you doing?"

"I know this isn't our real threshold, but still, I'm a traditional type of bloke."

He marched over the sand, holding me tight. The sound of his bare feet hit the smooth driftwood, and I tucked my face into his neck, breathed in the salt-laced scent of his sun-warmed skin.

"Let me," I said, when he struggled to hold me and unlock the door. I took the key and twisted it, tugged at the handle.

Ruben caught it with his foot, kicked it wide then stepped into the darkening villa. The door slammed behind us. "Here we are, Mrs. Strong. Welcome to your Barbados home."

"I was here earlier," I said, running my fingers through his hair and grinning

"Yes, but you weren't Mrs. Strong then. Now you are."

"And proud to be. Very proud." I pulled him in for a kiss.

He set me down and held me close. When he began to slip my thin dress straps from my shoulders, I pushed him away. "Ah, ah, no, no."

"But it's my right." He grinned. "You're mine. All mine."

I wagged my finger. "Naughty Mr. Strong. Go and get on the bed."

For a second I thought he wasn't going to do as I'd asked, but then he whipped off his shirt, tossed it on a wicker chair and moved to the imposing four-poster bed that dominated the room.

I turned and faced the dressing table and began to unpin my hair, performing my task slowly and knowing full well he'd be getting harder by the second. Each pin I dropped onto the shiny surface of the table allowed another tendril of my hair to fall loose.

When my style was down, tickling my shoulders, I reached behind myself and tugged the zip on my low-backed dress. Once released, I let the material shimmy down my hips and legs, revealing my white underwear. The bra was a corset, but a soft, comfortable one. The knickers were thong, and I treated him to a good view of my buttocks as I bent and retrieved my dress, staying stooped for a fraction longer than necessary.

Straightening, I caught his reflection. He was watching my every move, with his lips slightly parted. I noticed his attention kept returning to the white garter with a small blue bow that circled my right thigh.

I removed the silver necklace my parents had bought me to wear for the day, set it next to the pins. The tiny crinkling noise the chain made was loud in our silent room.

A swarm of desire took off inside me. It would have been easy to rush, to persuade him to jump onto my bandwagon of rampant lust, but I wanted it slow. Wanted this to be as special and treasured a memory as when we'd first made love.

I opened the small drawer beneath the table, took out my birth control pills. Turned and held them up.

"In the bin," he said, "as we planned."

A tiny wastepaper basket sat at my feet. I let go of the strip of foil, half full of yellow tablets, and let it flutter to the bottom of the plastic lining.

Done. As simple as that.

"Come here," he said. "Let's make love. Let's make babies."

"Let's make memories." I sashayed to the bed, rolling my hips suggestively, and my breasts moving a little in my corset. "But first you have a job to do."

"I like the sound of that."

I set my foot on the bed, twanged my garter. "I think tradition demands that you remove this with your teeth."

He licked his lips. "Well, it's a dirty job, but I suppose someone's got to do it, and like I said, I'm a traditional bloke."

He maneuvered into position, captured the lace frill in his teeth and dragged it down and over my knee. I studied his nose that had a sprinkle of freckles from the sun. The feel of his breath, the touch of his hair on my skin, it made impatience bubble within me again, but half the fun was keeping it protracted. Lingering over every move, every detail, every sensation.

He paused halfway down my calf and kissed my thigh where the garter had been—kisses as tiny as diamonds—then resumed his task, not cheating until it got looped on my toes.

"How is that?" he asked, holding it up with one finger.

"Perfect."

He set the garter on the bedside table then slipped off his chinos and boxers. "I have a wife," he said, reaching for my hand and pulling me onto the bed with him. "I'm so excited that I can say, my wife this and my wife that. My wife and I are going…"

"You can say all of those things, husband."

He grinned and tugged me down next to him. He lay on his side, half over me, and when I bent the leg opposite him, he sent his hand on a gentle drift from my ankle to hip and back again.

"I know sometimes we get a little wild," he said, kissing my cheek, "and I bloody love it. But tonight I just want to make love to you. I just want to be as close as two people can possibly be."

"That's what I want too," I said, feeling his cock press against my leg, the smooth head already a little filmy with desire. "That's what I want more than anything."

Together we discarded my thong, but I kept my pretty, wedding-night corset on as he moved over me. I reached for his firm buttocks and twined my legs around his. He slipped his arms beneath my shoulders, held me firmly then found my entrance and pushed in on a long, blissful glide.

Our lips hovered a hair's-breadth apart as our stuttered sighs and moans combined in a delicious melody of bliss.

"Katie?"

"Oh…oh, that's it." The feeling inside me was so perfect, he was touching just the right place, the end of his cock bumping over my sweet spot then burying deep and good.

"Katie, this heart that beats in my chest…"

"Ruben." I slid my hand up his back, taking in every dip and curve of his sinewy muscles. "Shh…"

"No, I understand it now, perfectly." He pulled out, smoothed back in. He was staring down at me with sudden urgency.

I coiled my fingers in the hair at the nape of his neck, the over-long tendrils that were perfect for hanging on to. "What? What do you understand?" I gasped.

His breath was warm and sweet and washed over me as he spoke. "This heart was made to love you, Katie, and you alone. Wherever it is, it beats only for you."

About the Author

Lily Harlem lives in the UK with a workaholic hunk and a crazy cat. With a desk overlooking rolling hills her over active imagination has been allowed to run wild and free and she revels in using the written word as an outlet for her creativity.

Lily's stories are made up of colourful characters exploring their sexuality and sensuality in a safe, consensual way. With the bedroom door left wide open the reader can hang on for the ride and Lily hopes by reading sensual romance people will be brave enough to try something new themselves? After all, life's too short to be anything other than fully satisfied.

Lily Harlem loves to hear from readers. You can find her contact information, website details and author profile page at http://www.totallybound.com.

Totally Bound Publishing